Dark
DESIRES
BLACK HOODS MC#4

Dark Desires

One night destroyed everything.

Lindsey's heart.

Karma's body.

Her hopes for the future are shattered. His purpose in the Black Hoods MC is unclear.

They thought they could weather any storm as long as they had each other. But some storms are too powerful. And some loves aren't as strong as they may seem.

Dedication

To our readers.

Sorry about the cliffhanger at the end.

Just kidding.

No, we're not.

MUAHAHAHAHAHA!

Chapter 1

LINDSEY

"PLEASE." The word slips past my lips in a whimper before I can stop it. Normally, that would result in a punishment for speaking without his permission, but I don't even care.

Wrapping his hand around the back of my neck, he pushes my face into the mattress, forcing me to suck in as much air as I can before he thrusts himself inside of me.

"God, yes," I moan.

It's been weeks since I've felt him. Weeks since I thought I'd lost him. Weeks since my world was hurled into a grand shit storm that's altered the course of everything in my life.

Curving his body over mine, our tattered hearts feel as if they're mending with every lustful breath.

"Jesus, Lins."

He feels it too. I know he does.

From the moment our eyes met across the smoky clubhouse of the Black Hoods MC, the connection between Karma and me had been instant. I was his, and he was mine. Though when we were shot, I thought we were ruined, and sometimes still do. But how could something so all-consuming and intense turn to ruin?

Thrusting my hips back, I whisper, "Faster," not giving him a choice. Karma likes control. He needs it. It's what we crave.

But right now, I'm just craving him.

Karma slides his hands down my body and digs his fingers into my hips. "Lindsey," he growls down at me. "Stop."

It definitely isn't the first time I've disobeyed him. When I do, it usually pushes us closer to the edge.

"Slow down," he grunts.

Desperate to reach orgasm, I move faster.

His body stiffens. Muttering something I can't make out, he releases his hold and goes soft inside of me, no longer aroused.

Oh my God.

Hot tears flood my eyes as he pulls away without a word. With my ass propped up in the air, I listen to him grab his jeans from the floor and pad out of the bedroom.

Remaining motionless until the door to the bathroom clicks shut, I collapse.

The tears fall before my face hits the mattress. I don't know if it's my pride or fear of wounding his, but I bite the comforter to muffle my sobs, keeping the hurt I feel to myself.

I don't understand it. It's been so long since we last touched each other, let alone made love. My body is always hungry for his, yet his is rejecting mine.

My hand flutters down to the scar on my belly, a constant reminder of all that's left of my womanhood. I lost more than just my ability to have children that day, I'd lost my baby—our baby. And now, I can't help but feel like I'm losing him.

From outside the room, he tells me, "I'm gonna head to the clubhouse for a while."

I hold my breath before breathing out slowly, making sure my voice is even when I reply with, "Okay."

"Be back soon," he murmurs while heading toward the door. Listening to him put on his boots, the door creaks open and slams closed with a thud. A few seconds later, his truck starts up in the driveway and takes off down the road, Karma's heavy metal music blaring through the speakers, and then silence.

Looking over at the clock to see it's four o'clock in the morning, my heart cracks a little more. Not exactly a normal time to be going out anywhere. What he should have said was, *"I need to get as far away from you as I can."*

Rolling onto my back, I wrap my arms around myself and stare up at the ceiling. This time, I don't muffle anything. When the tears come, I let them fall and sob uncontrollably.

What's happening to us?

KARMA

I'M A FUCKING ASSHOLE. I take what I want and push people to their limits by pure instinct, inflicting my wrath on my target until they give me what I want —submission.

The day Lindsey walked into the clubhouse was the day the beast inside of me staked his claim. Because of who her uncle was, she was forbidden fruit, and I was the kind of man who wanted to take a bite, no matter the consequences.

I wanted to break that wild spirit of hers, watch her come undone beneath me in pleasure. Showing up at our club under her uncle's watch meant one of two things: she either had no place to go, or she was a victim. For her, it was the latter, and we took care of that fucking problem within hours. And by we, I mean me. He wouldn't be a threat to her anymore, but she needed time to heal and to grow up. I had no choice but to wait until she was ready.

So I waited, watching her from the sidelines, all while keeping any man who threw a look her way off of her. If she only knew, it wasn't just her uncle who was keeping the little pissants from overstepping. Ironic, really, knowing the second she turned eighteen, I'd be the one chasing her, pulling us both so far under, there would never be anyone else for either of us. I had her walking a path she never knew she was on until I was sure she could handle everything I wanted to give her.

Little did I know how rocky that path would be, with her teasing, wanting me to take her at every opportunity. But I knew if I did and she wasn't ready, it would be a quick end to the plans I had for her. The long game was the only option. Years of back and forth, watching her parade around little fuck boys from college just to taunt me into action nearly killed me. Then, I snapped and made my move. After that, the rest was history. She was mine.

When she found out she was pregnant, I was truly happy for the first time in my life. Growing up with an abusive father, I felt like I was being given a chance to have a real, loving family with Lindsey and our baby. The one I never thought I deserved. Our child was my salvation from the darkness living inside of me.

Until Henry Tucker took it all away.

I'd had a ten percent chance of waking up, and the fact that I was still here was a miracle, according to the doctor. There are days I wish I hadn't. Wishing that instead of me, our child would have made it.

Now I'm just a broken man, trying to hold his woman together, and failing miserably.

If I had the balls, I'd admit out loud that I've been going through the motions, pretending to be happy about being alive, and that the loss of our child didn't affect me as much as it did Lindsey, all for her sake. But today, feeling her tight pussy wrapped around my cock for the first time in weeks, the paltry hold I'd had on my emotions unraveled. Subjecting her to my dark spiral wasn't an option, so I left.

I'm breaking her in the worst way, and I don't know how to stop the damage I'm inflicting on the fragile hold she has on her mental stability. She deserves more than this. She deserves the family she's always wanted to replace her lack of one. But being with me took that away.

Shoving my large frame into my truck, I run like a fucking coward and head for the clubhouse. It'll be quiet this time of night, or morning, and that's exactly what I need.

The farther away from the house I get, the more air I can suck into my lungs, albeit labored. Reduced lung capacity, the doctor had said. Lengthy recovery. Words that fuck with my head the more I replay them. I can't ride. I can't do the shit I need to do for my club. I'm just fucking breathing and taking up a seat at the table I don't deserve.

The weathered exterior of the clubhouse soothes the storm inside of me, like the touch of a good woman. Parking near the back door, I slip out of the truck and head inside, cringing when the door groans. Apparently, clubhouse maintenance has gone by the wayside in the last few weeks. Fucking prospects.

The place is as quiet as a sinner in church. Just the way I like it. Most of the guys have their own places, only staying here when their old ladies are pissed at them, or they're too drunk to go home. Or, in my case, seeking solitude.

I saunter over to the bar and find one thing hasn't changed. The fridge is stocked to the brim with amber bottles from various breweries. Grabbing the first one I see, I twist off the cap and slide onto a stool at the bar. Taking a swig, I let the cold liquid spill down my throat. Damn, it's been too long since I've had one of these. Between the pain meds, and Lindsey breathing down my neck, my house has become a dry county.

"Isn't it a little early for a beer?" a voice nags from behind me. I don't even have to look to know it's Hashtag. Of all the people to be around when you don't want them to be, he sure has a knack for it.

"You supposed to be drinking those meds of yours?" he inquires.

"You get a medical degree while I was gone?" I fire back.

"You wanna play doctor? I'm sure there's a nurse's outfit around here somewhere." I know the fucker's smiling at his own joke. The old me would've laughed and told him to shut the fuck up, but I can only muster up a grunt.

Sliding onto the stool next to me, he places a manila folder down in front of him. "Someone's a grump ass today. Not that it's any different from any other day."

"You planning on sitting there and busting my balls all day? Don't you have some computer shit to do?"

"My work can wait. Judge won't be here for another few hours, now that he's all familied up. Unlike other people who haven't done shit since Henry Tucker."

His words hit me like another gunshot to the chest. I grimace, and he catches my reaction instantly.

"Shit, man, I didn't mean it like that. Conversation this early isn't my strong suit."

Hash means well, I know he does, but he's not wrong in his observation. Everyone has their role to play. Techie shit for him. Leader for Judge. Peacemaker for Mom. General assholery for Stone Face. Enforcing for me. GP seems to be doing more cowboy shit than anything these days.

"It's fine, Hash. I know what you meant."

An awkward silence falls between us. The silence I came here for and haven't fucking got. He shifts on the stool next to me, itching to keep the conversation going.

"Out with it," I growl.

"You good? Don't think I've ever seen you here this early without an order from Judge."

"I'm fine."

"Doesn't sound like you're fine. Something up with you and Lindsey?"

"Drop it," I warn. My body grows rigid at the mention of her name, reminding me of the mess I'd left back at our place. The mess I'm going to have to deal with as soon as I get home, unless her uncle and my president don't kill me first. The talk he's been threatening to have with me about my relationship with his niece is long overdue, and frankly, I've been avoiding it, like a whole lot of other shit.

"Did Priest drive you?"

"You mean the shadow Judge put on me?"

"He's there to help you out. To keep you safe while you're healing. Where's he at, anyway?"

My safety. Before all this happened, I was the man you needed to be kept safe from. Now, I have a fucking babysitter in the form of a prospect.

"Probably asleep outside the house."

Surprise and concern crosses his face. "You drove here?"

"I have a license and everything," I sneer. "You wanna see it, Officer?"

"I get it, man, you're hurting. So are the rest of us. We nearly lost you. Pushing yourself this fucking hard isn't going to make shit go away. You need to take it easy and listen to that overpaid prick with a medical degree."

The monster inside of me moves from prickling under the surface to spilling over the edge before I can stop him. Tensing, I curl my fists and jump off the stool, knocking it to the floor.

"You don't know jack shit about what I went through, or what I lost to protect our club. Just leave me the fuck alone."

Grabbing my beer from the bar top, I leave his ass sitting there as I head toward the back door. If I can't find peace here, I'll never find it again.

Chapter 3

LINDSEY

KARMA STILL ISN'T HOME when I wake up the next morning. And when I check my phone, there's no text or calls from him, either.

Part of me is angry. I did nothing to warrant him walking out on me in the middle of the night, and I certainly did nothing to piss him off enough to stay gone and not contact me. But there's another part of me—a very sad, broken part—that wants to curl up in a ball and cry.

All of this, it's just too much.

I've known Karma since he first started prospecting with the Black Hoods MC. I wasn't much more than a kid back then—barely sixteen years old. But I knew the moment I laid eyes on Cyrus Kane, we belonged together. At the time, he wouldn't even consider it. To him, I wasn't only a kid, but I was the president of the

MC's niece. Two huge issues that made me more than just off-limits. It made me forbidden.

But eventually, I grew up, and I know he watched me do it. I noticed how he squirmed a little the first time I wore a bikini on our annual trip to the lake. I also saw the goosebumps race along the back of his neck the first time he gave me a ride home on the back of his motorcycle. I was a few weeks away from turning eighteen then. Feeling brave, I'd leaned forward and placed a featherlight kiss on his neck, just below his ear. He wanted me, but he would never admit it. Not then, anyway.

Once I turned eighteen, I pulled out all the stops in trying to earn Karma's affection. Nevertheless, he wasn't having it, and a girl can only take so much rejection before she finally gives up.

It wasn't until I started going out to bars and dating different men that Karma decided it was time to step up. I can't lie, I had fun leading him on a little chase. But after all he'd put me through, I was going to make him work for it.

And he did. He pursued me, then dominated me, and I loved every single minute of it. We kept it a secret for a long time, having too much fun sneaking around. But fun or not, we belonged to each other. We loved each other. And then, that fucker shot us both, leaving us twisted up and different, and I don't know how to feel or behave it seems.

What I do know is, I got hurt too. I can't ever recover what I lost that night. I lost our unborn child. I lost the ability to ever have children. So while my injuries and losses hadn't taken as long to physically recover from, I fucking lost a hell of a lot too.

So why is he walking out on me, like I don't understand it?

Angry now, I flip the covers off and stomp into the bathroom, continuing my rant as I go about getting ready for the day.

Does he think he's the only one who's suffered? Does he not realize how little I'd focused on my own emotional pain to help him recover?

I'm still pissed as I jump in my car and head for the university. I'm in my very last year, and dealing with Karma's bullshit isn't going to keep me from getting my doctorate. I've worked too damn hard for it.

The day drones on, seeming to take forever, with no contact from Karma. The fact that I haven't heard from him has my mind reeling. Is he okay? What happened last night, anyway? He just... deflated.

Is he not attracted to me anymore?

I snort a little at that. I know for a fact he's still attracted to me. My friend Blair and I have been taking kickboxing classes, and my body's tighter than it's ever been. I look freaking fantastic.

So if attraction isn't the issue, maybe he's just not in love with me anymore.

That thought is the one that makes my heart sink into my stomach and sit like a brick for the rest of the day. I go through the motions of going to classes and answering questions. I take a test I very likely failed. And when it's all done, I get in my car and drive home after the last class without remembering a single second of my commute.

When I pull into my driveway, another brick joins the first one in my stomach. Karma's truck is still gone. The only vehicle in the driveway is his motorcycle, which is currently covered up with a tarp because he hasn't used it since... well, not since that night.

I walk up to our small two-bedroom house and unlock the door. Inside is tidy, as usual, but not overly inviting. Karma had lived at the clubhouse before he was hurt, and I'd lived in a shared student apartment.

After we were both released from the hospital, we'd moved into this place with what little furniture we had. It isn't much, but it's ours. The plan is to make this into a home, together.

A third brick joins the other two, and the sadness of the situation nearly knocks me over.

What's happening to us? This isn't what I envisioned when I'd fantasized about my life with Karma all those years ago.

Deciding to bite the bullet, I send him a text.

When do you think you'll be home?

There. Now he'll answer, and I'll finally be able to breathe when I know when to expect him.

That tiny bit of relief doesn't last long, because he doesn't respond. I'd apparently sent that text out into the atmosphere, and I don't even know if he read it. But if he did, he didn't feel it necessary to respond.

A fourth brick clatters in with the other three, and I can't take it anymore. I can't hold back the tears or the pain. None of this is what's supposed to be happening. None of this is what I ever wanted.

Not caring that it's only six o'clock in the evening, I dress in my comfiest pajamas and brush my teeth before crawling into bed, silently weeping through the entire routine. It's not until I grab Karma's pillow, with the scent of him embedded in every single fiber, that my silent tears change.

My chest heaves with great wracking sobs as I cling to it.

Should I text him again?

Absolutely not. I won't start kissing his ass for attention.

But why won't he just come home?

That's the thought that lingers as I cry myself to sleep.

Chapter 4

KARMA

THE SPRING SUN batters down on me as I aim my side piece at a couple of beer bottles lined up along the makeshift gun range out back. It's my peaceful escape since this morning's run-in with Hashtag. The guys came and went all day, but no one bothered me back here. A good thing for us all, considering the anger swirling inside of me. I line up my shot and fire, the blast echoing off the buildings surrounding me. It misses its target. The recoil sends a painful jolt up my arm and I hiss in pain.

"Fucking useless," I berate myself. I can't even fucking fire a gun. Let's just add that to the other things on the can't-do shit list.

My phone vibrates in my pocket. Pulling it out, I find another message from Lindsey, this one more desperate than the last dozen or so she's sent me since I left this morning.

Please, Karma, text me back. Tell me you're okay.

My chest aches at the thought of what she must be feeling. I know she's worried, but me coming home right now isn't going to do either of us any good. Another fight will solve nothing, only further the hurt I'm inflicting on her. It's what's best.

I go to type out a quick reply when the loud roar of bikes pulling into the parking lot gains my attention. Peering down at the time on my phone, I see it's six o'clock. Time for church. Flipping quickly to the club's group text, I realize I have no notifications. Those fuckers have cut me out.

Slipping my gun into the holster at my hip, I trudge toward the building and fling open the metal door, getting the attention from everyone in the room, all looking at me like I'm some fucking outsider.

"You meeting without me now?" I shout as Judge steps out of the meeting room. If possible, his hair is even grayer now, but his cold eyes are always the same.

"You're on leave," he curtly reminds me with a hardened stare. "Go home."

"Fuck that. I *am* a member of this club."

He charges toward me with a look in his eyes I've only seen a few other times in the years I've been in this club.

Stopping just inches away from me, he orders, "Go

home. You're injured. Until that overpaid doctor clears you, you're benched."

I don't back down. Going home is not an option until I figure out how to cool down the shit storm I left there with Lindsey.

"Not fucking moving."

"You nearly died, Karma."

"Yet here I am," I retort, lifting my arms in the air.

"I'm not about to put you back into the field when you're not ready.

"I am ready." Lies. All fucking lies. But sitting around on my ass is getting old. The bullshit physical therapy appointments the doctor keeps booking for me sure as fuck aren't going to help. If I want to get back to the way things were, I have to get back to work.

"Put me to work. Give me something." My appeal comes out as more of an angry demand than a request.

Judge shakes his head in frustration, rubbing his large hand down his face.

"I get it. You want to protect me, but I'm not the kind of man who sits on the fucking sidelines when my brothers have business to handle. I know you don't think I'm ready, but the only way I will be is if I get back to work. Use me."

"What about my niece?"

"This is best for both of us. We need fucking normalcy, Judge."

That makes him pause. "Fine. But you're still grounded. No fights, and no cowboy shit. You stay back when I tell you to. Understood?"

"Yeah," I relent with a relieved sigh. It's not entirely what I want, but it's something.

Without another word, he pivots on his heel and heads back into the meeting room, with the rest of us following along behind him. A sense of contentment and familiarity washes over me when I sit down in my chair for the first time in weeks. Taking a moment to peer around the room, I notice Stone Face, Mom, and Twat Knot are missing. Being absent from a meeting like this seems odd. They're mandatory, so what the fuck?

Judge bangs the gavel, bringing the meeting to order.

"For those of you who aren't aware, the string of break-ins at the new garage continues."

"How many times has this happened?" I inquire.

"Four by last count."

I frown. Four break-ins, and we hadn't stopped them yet? What the hell is really going on here? Guys missing. People taking our shit. We'd be busting skulls after the first one, so why the hesitation now?

"The cameras I installed last week had the wires cut."

"What about the feeds?" GP asks. "Surely, they picked up something."

"Absolutely fucking nothing."

"How is that fucking possible?" I interject. "It's a camera. That's what it's supposed to do, isn't it?"

"These guys have to be professionals. They figured out the blind spots and stayed in the shadows. I thought I had every square inch of the place covered, but they found a way around them."

I shake my head in disbelief. We're the Black Hoods MC, for fuck's sake. Shit like this doesn't happen to us. Our reputation alone should send thieves running for their lives. Either the people behind this are incredibly brazen, or they're outsiders who don't know who they're fucking with.

"What exactly are we going to do about it?"

"We're working on that, Karma. But until we figure out who these guys are and why they're targeting our new garage, we're in a holding pattern," Hashtag offers.

"Holding pattern? When the fuck did we ever do that? Did shit change while I was in the hospital?"

"A lot of things changed, Karma. We're dealing with it," Judge adds before turning back to the skeleton crew in the room. "Anything else?" When no one replies, Judge shoves away from the table. Meeting over, I guess.

I wait around until everyone funnels out, leaving just the two of us in the room.

"When did meetings become optional?" I ask, watching his body go rigid.

"You're not the only one dealing with some shit, Karma. We all have our own problems."

I raise my brow. "Like what?"

"You've got enough on your plate."

"Bullshit. I said put me to work. Tell me what's going on."

He starts to open his mouth, but V, one of the prospects, knocks on the door.

"Someone's here asking for you, Prez. Couple of old guys."

"Expecting company?" I ask Judge.

Stepping around the table, he shakes his head as he exits the room with me hot on his heels. At the front door of our clubhouse is Priest, flanked by three elderly men whose worn faces and stained jean overalls contrast greatly against their surroundings.

One of the men steps forward and announces, "Name's Bill Henry. This here is Gus Masterson and Harold McCombs."

"I'm Judge. What exactly can I do for you gentleman?"

"Heard you're having the same problem with your repair shop as we are."

"That so?" Judge grunts.

"Yes, sir. We've all been hit a couple of times now. Tools stolen. Cars stripped down to the metal."

"I see." Judge shows no reaction, but I know him. He's playing it cool.

"These businesses are our livelihoods."

"Why not go to the police?"

"We have, and that's why we're here. We're done watching from the sidelines while everything we've worked for gets stolen out from under us."

Judge relaxes. Guys like these are a dying breed. They came from nothing, scraped by to make ends meet and make something of themselves, and they're still doing it this late in life because it's the only way they know and respect. Roughnecks until their dying breath.

"I'm not sure how much we can help, but why don't you three come in and take a seat, and we'll see what you have to say."

Chapter 5

LINDSEY

THE SUN SHINING through the open curtains is what wakes me. I yawn and roll over, but opening my eyes isn't as easy as it should be.

And then the blissful oblivion of sleep disappears as I remember what's been going on. I look over to Karma's side of the bed, finding it untouched.

Snatching my phone off the nightstand, I sit up and open my text thread with Karma. No replies.

My heart plummets, and my anger is overshadowed by fear. What if something happened to him? What if he's been hurt? He wouldn't do something to…

I shake my head, because no, that would never happen. Not Karma.

So what's the deal, then?

Closing the chat thread, I open my contact list and

call my uncle. It rings several times before going to voicemail.

If anyone would know where Karma is, it would be Uncle Judge. But if he's not answering his phone, it means he's got it turned off.

Maybe his girlfriend knows something.

I try her number next. Grace and my uncle have only been together for a short time, and I admit, I wasn't much of a fan at first. She's the exact opposite of him, but I think that may be what makes them such a great match. They even each other out.

That thought makes me sad. I used to think Karma and I evened each other out, but now that we're on such shaky ground, I can't help but wonder if we were a mistake from the start.

Grace answers the phone on the second ring, pulling me from that depressing thought.

"Hello?"

I force myself to smile, knowing she can't see it, but I don't want to sound like my heart's caving in on itself.

"Hey, Grace. I was wondering if you know where my uncle is? He's not answering his phone, and I have something kind of important to talk to him about."

"He was having one of his church meetings this evening, and he always turns his phone off for that. He was also planning on going to the garage to do inventory and order supplies."

"Oh, okay. Well, if you talk to him, can you tell him to call me? And tell him it's important."

"Okay," Grace says, now sounding worried. "Is everything all right with you, Lins? You sound... sad."

Tears burn behind my eyelids as I swallow.

"Yeah. I just haven't heard from Karma, and I'm getting a little worried."

"Haven't heard from him? What do you mean? Since when?"

I swallow, trying to hold myself together. "Yesterday morning."

At her silence, I can feel my pulse beating in my throat.

"Jeez," Grace huffs. "I don't even know what to say. I'll have your uncle call you as soon as I speak with him."

"Thanks," I reply in a shaky voice.

"Do you want to come over? Maybe have a cup of tea?"

I smile. Judge may be my uncle, but he feels more like a father. Though Grace may be new to their relationship, she's beginning to fill out the mother role better than I expected.

"I'm good. I'm going to keep searching for Karma. Thank you, though."

"Well, you let me know when you find him. And if he's still alive, kick his ass. That's unacceptable."

"I will," I whisper, my gut twisting into a knot. "Talk soon."

Hanging up, I wrap my arms around my waist, as if that'll keep me from falling to pieces. I don't want to be Lindsey, the girl who could never be put back together again.

When my phone rings, I jump, bringing it close to see if it's Karma. It's not.

Putting the phone to my ear, I answer, "Hi, Blair."

"Well don't sound so excited about it," she teases.

Sighing, I flop back onto the bed. "Sorry. I thought maybe you were Karma."

"Karma? Why? What's going on?"

I tell her. I tell her about how moody he's been lately, and about the other night. It feels good to tell someone, to talk about it, especially with Blair.

We both attend the same university, and even have the same major. That's how we met and became friends. But then Blair met GreenPeace, and they fell in love, making her his fiery red-haired old lady. That's how we became sisters.

"So he just walked out on you?" she sputters in disbelief. "In the middle of buttering your muffin?"

"Yep."

"Did you even get yours?"

"Blair!" I squeal through a laugh.

"I'm just asking is all," she giggles. "Anyway… Yes,

I admit, that's an asshole move. But you and I both know there's a lot going on below the surface with your man."

"I know," I groan. I don't have to like it, but she's right.

"Karma loves you, Lins, you know that. If anyone can help him through whatever this is, it's you."

I sigh, feeling a little better already. "I know that too."

"But this whole taking off and no contact for two whole nights? That's a no-no. He can be going through his shit, but he can go through it and still respect your feelings. If you don't remind him of that, I will."

She would too. "Thanks, Blair."

"And that brings me to why I called. Something's going down over at the clubhouse, but GP didn't tell me what. He just told me they were men on a mission and needed sustenance. I told him to order a damn pizza. I won't tell you what he said next."

I chuckle. "I can only imagine."

"Anyway, I'm going to head over and make them some sandwiches, and was wondering if you wanted to tag along? I bet Karma's there."

She doesn't have to ask me twice. I agree to meet her and end the call before hopping out of bed. I make a piss poor effort to conceal the dark circles under my eyes, brush my teeth, throw my hair up in a messy bun, and grab my comfiest yoga pants and T-shirt.

By the time Blair shows up ten minutes later, I'm ready to go.

"Jeez, girl. You look like shit," she tells me once I'm seated next to her.

"Bite me."

She grins. "No thanks. You're not my flavor, sweet cheeks."

And for just a second, I forget about the painful hole in my chest and laugh. Blair giggles beside me, reminding me of how thankful I am to have her.

Once our laughter dies down, she looks at me with a serious expression. "What are you going to do if he's there?"

"Rip his balls off," I say in a matter-of-fact tone, but I follow it up with a sigh, because truthfully, I don't know how to answer that question. "I guess it'll be a surprise for the both of us."

We spend the rest of the short drive to the MC's clubhouse in silence. But as we pull in, the sound of my heartbeat galloping at a pace that may just cause me to have a heart attack drowns it out.

Karma's standing by the entrance, a bottle of beer in one hand and a cigarette in the other.

"Oh, shit," Blair mutters.

She's barely parked the car before I'm scrambling out of it. Even as I approach him, I still don't know what I'm going to say.

But when I get to him, he only stares back at me with empty eyes. He doesn't say a word, either. No apology for taking off, and no explanation for ghosting me these past few days.

"What the fuck, Karma?" I cry, the words pouring from the very depths of my battered soul. "Where the hell have you been? Why haven't you called, or at least fucking texted!"

"Uh-oh," Twat Knot quips from a few feet away. "Looks like Karma's about to get his balls busted."

"Fuck you," I seethe, whipping around to point a finger at him. "And before I have to say it,"—I swing my finger toward Burnt and one of the prospects—"fuck you too. This is between me and him, so beat it."

Burnt holds his hands up in surrender and slowly backs away, while Priest turns and walks in the other direction. Twat Knot, on the other hand, never knows when to quit.

"Jeez, woman. Don't shit a chicken. I was just trying to lighten the mood."

"Beat it," Karma snarls before I get a chance to reply. "Now."

Twat Knot values his life, because he disappears in a hurry. Blair mutters a quick "Excuse me," as she scurries inside with a load of shopping bags, and then we're alone.

I turn to him again, slightly less pissed now, and

happy to see him unharmed. "When did you start smoking again?"

"Yesterday."

I don't like that at all, but it's not important right this second. "Where have you been, Karma?"

"Here."

"Why weren't you answering my calls or texts?"

His brows draw together. "Since when are you my mother?"

My anger is building again. Quickly. "It's common courtesy, Karma. If you're not going to be home, you call or text, especially after walking out on me in the middle of—"

"Shut. Up." Grabbing my arm, he spins me around and presses my back against the brick wall.

"Nobody's out here. Nobody can hear us."

Releasing me, he backs away. "I don't fucking care. Just keep your mouth shut."

In all the time I've known him, Karma has never spoken to me this way. No man has. My uncle would string their balls around their ears and call them earrings if they even tried.

All I can do is gape at him, my body trembling in anger.

"I've been here, at the clubhouse, okay? That's all you need to know. I'm not some kid who needs to check in with you every fifteen fucking minutes, Lindsey. And right now, I need space, so why don't you go home?"

Just then, Judge opens the door and heads toward us, pointing at the security camera to our left.

"Gotta tell ya, I'm not liking one fucking thing I just saw on that camera."

I watch in shock as Karma tosses his cigarette and pushes past my uncle, muttering, "Fuck this."

"When will you be home?" I call out.

"When I fucking get there!"

And then he's gone.

Judge doesn't say a word, knowing me better than that. Instead, he walks over and envelops me in his massive arms.

I will not fall apart. I will not fall apart.

"You gonna tell me what's going on here, kiddo?"

I shake my head, swallowing back the lump in my throat.

"You want me to take you home?"

I nod.

Letting me go, Judge takes my hand, walks me to his motorcycle, and takes me home.

Chapter 6

KARMA

THE SECOND JUDGE comes back from taking my girl home, he makes a beeline straight for me with his fist aimed in the direction of my face. I could duck, even swing back, but everything behind that rage in his grasp is warranted, and hits me square in the jaw. I stumble back from the force, but catch myself before I lose my balance.

My hand goes to my jaw and cracks it back into place. He eyes me, anticipating if I'm stalling in striking back, but I reach down and grab my beer from the table instead. The man may be older than me, but fuck, he still packs a punch. I'm lucky my jaw's not broken.

"Feel better?"

"Not in the fucking slightest. My office. Now."

He doesn't stick around to hear my answer, assuming his order will be followed.

TK smiles and shouts, "Dead man walking!" before humming some fucking death march song.

"Shut the fuck up," I growl at him.

Taking one last swig of my beer, I slam the bottle down and make the trek to Judge's office, each step feeling heavier than the last. This conversation was never going to be easy, but after Lindsey's surprise visit and ball-busting, it's upping the difficulty level from hard to fucking impossible.

The door is open when I approach. With a deep breath, I step inside, coming nose to nose with him.

"You and I need to get some fucking things straight, boy," Judge growls like a wild fucking animal, his hot breath blasting me in the face. I've seen this man kill, yet I've never seen him like this.

He may be twenty or so years older than me, but I'm nearly as big as he is. Even hurt, I could still take him down in a fight.

"Like what?"

"I don't like this shit between you and my niece. Doing it behind my back until you got her knocked up? I should've fucking killed you then. But if I ever see you lay a hand on her like that again, I'll put you in the fucking ground without so much as a shred of remorse," he threatens, his chest heaving with every word. Judge has precision control, and he's on the brink of losing it.

"Then why am I breathing?"

I want to agree, because I'd have said the same fucking thing if the roles were reversed. I'd have killed a man for the way I'd treated Lindsey tonight, but he's only seeing one side of the story.

"You done? Good talk."

I go to shove off from my spot, but he starts back in on me.

"Not even close. What the fuck is going on in that head of yours, Karma? It didn't take a rocket scientist to see this morning that something was up with you. I thought you were working some shit out because of your injuries, but this shit with my niece? I know there's something else going on."

"It's not your problem, Judge."

"The fuck it isn't!" he barks out. "That girl is like my daughter. I raised her for over half her life after my sister dumped her off and never looked back. I'm not fucking blind at my age to see she's unhappy and know what the root cause of it is."

I hesitate in my response. There's shit a man needs to know about his family, and shit he doesn't. If he truly knew the history between Lindsey and I, I'd be dead already.

"It's none of your business."

"You keep saying that shit, but you forget who I am. And let's not forget about you not coming to me when you started dating her. A real man would've done that, but you didn't, and now she's hurting. As her uncle, I have every fucking right to know why that is. As your president, I need to have a reason not to run your ass right out of this club for hiding this shit from me. I normally don't get involved in people's business, but this one's personal."

"I fucked up, okay," I admit out loud. "The other night, we got into it and I walked out."

"That explains the where, but I'm still waiting on the why."

"There's some shit a man doesn't need to know, Judge. Believe me, this is one of those things."

Judge crosses his arms over his chest. A challenge if I ever saw one, begging me to try him.

"Things haven't been great between us since I got home from the hospital."

"Tell me something I don't already know," he reminds me harshly. "That's not why you laid hands on her tonight."

I rake my hand through my hair. "It's not that easy to explain."

"Surviving what you did takes a lot out of man, but let's not pretend here that losing your baby isn't the real cause of this. It's not easy, K. Coming back from the brink and finding out you've lost your kid is enough to shut down any weak man's system. But you're not weak. You took a fucking bullet to the heart and you're still breathing. You're a fighter, Karma, but the man I know wouldn't have reacted the way he did tonight."

"I know. I fucked up."

"Damn right you did, but she's hurt too. Something you'd be wise to remember next time."

"That night's screwing with my head. It's like it's replaying over and over again." The first real truth slips from my lips before I can stop it, but a small pang of relief follows it.

"Losing a kid? It fucking hurts. You think of shit you should've never done, should've changed, but it doesn't change the fact that it happened. Death is the one final thing in this life. You have to forgive yourself for surviving. Both of you do. You can come back from it, but fighting the way you two are isn't going to make that easy. You need to talk to her, Karma. Really talk to her. She's hurting just as bad as you are. Maybe even worse."

He's right, I know this, but what do I say to her? Leaving her a few nights ago was one thing, but the shit I pulled tonight? I'll be lucky if she hasn't changed the locks on the house.

"Go home, Karma. Work this shit out."

"Is that an order?"

"Damn fucking right, it is."

With a nod, I leave his office. That could've ended a lot differently. I'll take it as a win that I'm still fucking breathing right now.

The peanut gallery in the main room goes quiet when I walk back out, all eyeing me. Not a peep comes out of their mouths when I stalk past them and out the back door, straight to my truck.

Palming my keys, I throw open the door and slide in behind the wheel where I sit for a few minutes, trying to figure out what I can do or say to fix the shit that went down earlier with Lindsey. I was out of line. No amount of flowers is gonna fix this shit.

Starting the ignition, I turn on the heat, seeing that the warmer air outside has fallen away to colder temperatures. Spring was a bitch like that in Texas. While I let the truck warm up, I pull out my phone and fumble out a quick text to Lindsey to tell her I'm coming home and that we need to talk. I watch as the three little dots pop up, but a reply never comes back.

Preparing for my clothes to be in a flaming heap in the front yard, I back out of my spot and start for the main entrance when I slam on the brakes at the silhouette of a person appearing in my headlights. I throw my truck in park and get out.

"The fuck you want?" I call out to the person shrouded in darkness just outside the gates. There's no reply. "I said, the fuck you want!" I yell a little louder this time, approaching slowly with my hand on the butt of my gun. The person staggers closer until the headlights shine directly on them.

An old man, bloody from his head to his torso, comes into view.

"Fuck," I hiss as I run—if you could call it running with my injuries—toward him. Watching him collapse, I hit the ground and pull his head up to rest on my knees.

"Please," he wheezes, his eyes pleading. "Please, help us."

Wiping the blood from his aged face, I realize why he's here. It's one of the men from yesterday who came looking for help. His breathing goes flat until he passes out in my arms.

Chapter 7

LINDSEY

HEADING HOME NOW. **We need to talk.**

That's what Karma's text had said, and that had been last night.

He didn't come home.

I'm way past anger now. After the way he spoke to me last night, the way he'd grabbed me, I'm near my breaking point.

"Lindsey, did you hear me?"

Blinking, I turn my focus back to the present. Professor McCallen is watching me with a concerned smile.

"Sorry. I have a lot on my mind."

Placing her elbows on the desk, she tents her fingers in front of her. "Your failing grade is concerning. You're usually an exemplary student who's close to graduating with honors. But this one failed test will change that."

My heart feels like it's shriveling inside my chest.

"I know you've been through so much these past few weeks. Have you been talking to someone? A professional?"

I shake my head. "I don't need to see a therapist."

Professor McCallen smiles, but it's a placating lift of her lips and no more.

"Lindsey, in all the years you've attended this school, you've never gotten less than an eighty-five percent on a test. Not once. So, I'm sure you can understand why seeing you get a mere forty-five percent is such a cause for concern."

Sighing, I slump back in my chair. "I know, and I'm sorry. Everything seems to be piling up on top of me, and I can't seem to balance any of it. I feel like my entire life is spinning out of control."

The professor leans forward and places her hand on the desk in front of me, her gaze capturing mine. "You're a strong woman, Lindsey. You've proven that time and time again, and this too will pass. Unfortunately for you, though, this test mark will not."

I bite the inside of my lip and blink away the tears that are threatening to spring forth.

Pushing back in her seat, she stands and rounds the desk, heading toward her office door. "Next Monday, eight o'clock in the morning, I'll allow you a retest. Just this one time, and just this one test."

Pushing to my feet, I clutch my books to my chest. "Oh, thank you, Prof—"

She raises her hand to stop me. "Don't thank me. Just pass it."

Swallowing back my relief, I take a step toward the door when she swings it open, clearly ready for me to leave.

"I will," I assure as I pass by her and into the hallway.

"And Lindsey?" I turn to see her kind eyes clouded with concern. "Talk to someone. Doesn't have to be me or anyone you know. Just find someone to help you work through this trauma objectively."

"Yes, ma'am."

With that, she closes her door and I head out of the building, straight for my car. I can't believe Professor McCallen is giving me another chance. I also can't believe I failed that fucking test. I never do that.

Not until Karma.

That's the thought that plays in my head the whole drive home. Karma has changed so much since he was shot, and that change is wreaking havoc on my heart. Hell, on my entire life.

He's like a different person entirely.

Anger boils through my veins. Anger at myself for failing that test. Anger at Karma for the way he's been behaving. Anger at the son of a bitch who'd shot us both in the first place. And anger that I'm angry at all.

I've never been an angry person. I hate feeling this way. I don't want this.

As I pull into my driveway, my stomach turns itself inside out. Karma's truck is here, parked in the driveway, as if he'd never left. And for a moment, all I feel is relief.

He's home, and he's safe.

I angle my car across the driveway, purposely blocking him in, and gather my things.

He's still the fucking asshole who blew me off yesterday, but I'm not going to let him do it today.

I step inside the house and drop my backpack and keys on the kitchen table. Silence pounds in my ears, accompanied by my own heartbeat.

A quick scan shows he's not on the main floor, so I start up the stairs, my blood pressure rising with each step.

The bathroom door stands ajar, and the rapid spray of the shower tells me exactly where he is.

Okay, Lins. What now?

I consider going into that bathroom and ripping him a new one while he shampoos his hair. But instead, I take a seat on the end of the bed facing the door, and I wait. He'll come in here to get dressed and make sure his towel gets thrown in a heap directly in front of the laundry hamper.

My blood pressure rises a little more.

A few seconds later, the water cuts off, and the

shower rings scrape along the metal rod. I listen to the quiet sounds of him stepping out and towel drying himself, and then his footsteps grow closer and closer.

"Jesus, baby," he barks as soon as he walks into the room. "Why the fuck are you sitting there like a damn statue? Scared the shit out of me."

"We need to talk."

Karma pauses for just a moment before nodding and moving toward his dresser, holding the towel in front of his junk as if I hadn't already seen it, licked it, sucked it and fucked it a million different ways already.

Snagging a pair of jeans out of the bottom drawer, he stabs one leg through, and then the other. It's not until he has them buttoned up and resting low on his hips that he turns to me and responds.

"Listen, Lins, I get you're pissed at me, but I—"

"I failed my test," I blurt out, popping up to my feet and standing directly in front of him. I allow my arms to hang down at my sides, but I can't help but curl my fists when I envision myself landing a right hook to his stupid, gorgeous face.

He frowns down at me. "What?"

"My psych test," I repeat. "I failed it because of you. Because of your bullshit and your attitude, and you being a total prick who doesn't have the common decency to pick up the goddamn phone and tell his girlfriend, whom he lives with, I might add, that he's okay."

"Baby, I—"

"I may not graduate," I continue. It's been days since he took off, and I have shit he needs to hear. If I don't get it off my chest now, it's going to crush me. "I've worked my ass off for years, and there's a chance I may not graduate, Karma. That too falls on you."

Karma straightens, and his demeanor changes. He's no longer in damage control mode. He's in defense mode.

"That's bullshit, and you fucking know it is."

My body is trembling now. I feel like I'm going to explode.

"Would you be okay with me just disappearing like that? Telling you I'll be home and not show up?"

Scoffing, he turns to dig a clean shirt out of his dresser. He's not even going to argue. I've seen this response from him a lot lately where he ignores me and walks away because I'm some irrational woman without any reason to be upset. But I've had it.

"What's going on here, Karma?" I ask the back of his head, to which he doesn't respond. "You left me while we were in the middle of sex, for fuck's sake." The muscles in his back stiffen, but he still doesn't say a word. "Are you not attracted to me anymore? Did I do something wrong? You owe me something after ghosting me like that."

Pulling his T-shirt on over his head, he starts rooting around in a different drawer for a pair of socks.

I know I need to calm down, but dammit, I want answers.

"Does it not work anymore?"

Karma spins around, his eyes wild and hard. "Yes, it still fucking works!" he shouts, his neck muscles straining with the effort. "Maybe it just doesn't want to work for you."

Silence follows as we glare at each other.

The closest thing to me right then is a hardcover book I'd been reading the other night. He's lucky it's not a blade, or a ninja star, or some other sharp object, because before I can stop myself, I snatch the book off the bedside table and hurl it at him.

The book bounces off his chest and falls to the floor with a thud.

"Fuck you," I mutter as I shove past him and out of the room.

I make it out to the car, knowing he won't bother coming after me. It's not his style.

I pull out my phone and text Blair.

SOS. Meet me at the clubhouse ASAP.

Chapter 8

KARMA

TALK TO HER. *Great fucking advice, Prez.*

Lindsey didn't have talking on her mind at all, except to tell me how much of an asshole I am and chucking that book at me. Talking was the last thing on her mind, and I really can't blame her. She has every fucking right to be pissed.

Yeah, I'd fucked up, but she wouldn't let me get a word in edgewise. No explanation. Just an ass ripping from her and then watching her taillights pulling away. I know there's people out there who say relationships are easy, but fuck me, they haven't been in one with my girl. She's got a big heart with a mean streak a mile long. Guessing she gets that from her uncle.

Stomping back to my truck, I pop open the driver's side door, slide inside, and grip the steering wheel so tight, the leather squeaks.

"Well, what the fuck do I do now?" I grumble to myself. I never should've said that last part, because all it did was make things worse. Going after her is the first thing I consider, but she needs time to calm the hell down. Knowing her as I do, she's probably already on Blair and GP's couch, venting to her best friend. I may not have been big on GP's old lady at first, but she really stepped it up to help us both after the accident. Blair's good people, and I'm glad Lindsey has a woman in her life now. She'd grown up around too many roughneck bikers, and fuck, does it show.

Fuck it. There's no point in staying here. Shoving my keys into the ignition, I pull away and drive. I don't know where I'm going, and I don't even think about it. It's like I'm on autopilot. The truck goes where I point it, but I'm not even really aware of where that is.

Then my ass starts to hurt. I can't just drive forever, anyway, and I can't exactly go home, so instead, I head toward the one place I know is always open. The clubhouse.

I let my mind drift during the drive, trying to figure out what I can do to fix this shit between Lindsey and I. That thought evaporates the second my headlights hit the back of her Toyota Corolla nestled between a row of bikers at the front entrance.

Every vein in my body constricts. She came here, not

to Blair's. Not to her uncle's new woman. She came to my fucking clubhouse.

I'm out of the truck before I can get my head on straight. I fling open the door, and what do I fucking see? Lindsey with a beer in her hand, tucked up between the two soon-to-be dead fucking prospects laughing it up with her.

V's face goes white when he spots me. Priest freezes, and Lindsey smiles at me like a child with a shiny new toy. She knew I'd come here.

"The fuck you think you're doing?" I yell at her, crossing the room in a brisk walk.

She looks to Priest and V, who scatter off the couch like it's on fire. If they'd have stayed, it would've, and I like that fucking couch. I've slept enough nights on it to know.

"What does it look like I'm doing?"

"It looks like you're in my fucking clubhouse having a fucking beer with two dead prospects. That's what it looks like to me, Lindsey."

"Your clubhouse?" she fires back, stretching her arms over the back of the couch. "You mean *my* clubhouse."

"The fuck it is."

"I'm family, jackass. What are you?"

The fuck did she just say? This is my club. My home. She may be family to Judge, but this club is the only family I got. Every drop of blood and sweat built into what it is comes from men like me. My brothers.

"This isn't a game, Lindsey."

"Don't you like games, Karma? You seem to get off on them lately."

"Knock it off," I growl. "This isn't the place for that shit."

Leaning her tight body forward, she shoves those gorgeous tits of hers front and center as she puts her bottle down on the table, all with a fucking grin on her face.

"Seems like it's the perfect place for this. You don't come home anymore, so I might as well come to you."

"Fucking hell, woman. Stop." This time, it comes out as a sneering command. Playtime is over.

Lindsey rises from the couch, staring me down, challenging me with every step. She gets within inches of me when the clack of heels comes up loudly from behind me.

"You both need to stop this right now!" Blair roars, stepping between us. "This doesn't solve a thing."

"Of course it does," Lindsey interjects without taking her eyes off of me.

"No, it doesn't," Blair snaps. "You both need to talk, and without a fucking audience. Pick a room and hash this out. It's eating you both up inside." I watch as a flicker of remorse flashes across Lindsey's face before she bristles up again. I couldn't agree more, but admitting it out loud would only set her off again.

"No thanks." Relaxing her shoulders, she looks to Blair. "I'd rather drink with you."

"It wasn't a request," Blair says, her voice a little harder now. Firmer. "Either you go on your own, or I'll go to Judge. Your choice."

Neither of us say a word, but I know I don't want Judge weighing in on any of this anymore.

Blair raises a brow in my direction. "Karma?"

"Yeah," I growl, giving in.

"Lindsey?"

"Fine," she huffs, folding her arms over her chest.

Blair grabs her by the hand and takes off toward the hallway where most of the bedrooms are. I follow behind until she stops outside of my room, the one I haven't stepped foot in since before the accident. The same room where Lindsey told me she was pregnant, the same night I got shot. Lindsey digs in her heels, looking over her shoulder at me.

"You need this, both of you. Please, for the sake of your relationship, and the club's sanity, talk."

Releasing Lindsey's hand, she stomps past me without so much as a second glance. We both stand there until the clack of her heels disappears.

"Not this room." I walk farther down to one of the rooms at the end of the hall. When Lindsey follows me inside, I close the door behind us. The air grows heavy with the deafening silence.

"This isn't going to work if we don't say anything," I say after a few moments pass.

"I have nothing to say to you."

"Yeah, you do, or you wouldn't have tried to take my head off earlier with that fucking book. Nice shot, by the way. I'm sure it'll leave a lovely bruise."

She frowns. I guess lightening the mood is going to do fuck all. Taking a deep breath, I let shit go.

"I've been an asshole, Lindsey, to everyone, but especially you."

She remains silent. If she doesn't want to talk, then she can sure as hell listen.

"I've been going through the motions for a few weeks now, trying to figure out where I fit into all this. Why I survived and our baby didn't. The other night, I finally felt like the man I was before…" My words trail off, not knowing how to say this.

"What about how I felt? You walked out and left me for days. No texts. No calls. No explanation. Just an empty side of the bed, and me to wonder what I did wrong."

When I take a few steps closer to her, she stiffens.

"You did nothing wrong. This is all on me. I wanted to give you what you needed. Fuck, what we both needed, and I just got too up in my head. I put so much pressure on being with you again that I couldn't, and that pissed me off. I didn't know how to face it, or you."

"You fucking talk to me, that's how you face it. You don't leave me there for days. The man I knew wouldn't have left like that. You're like a fucking stranger living in Karma's skin."

I drop my head at the shame and sorrow filling my insides.

"I know, sugar. That's on me. The other night, I thought I was okay, but I wasn't. I needed space. Then some shit happened with the club, and instead of dealing with the mess I left behind, I focused on something else when my focus should've been on you."

"Pretty words," she drawls. "If it was anyone but you saying that, you might have had me convinced. The truth is, things got tough, and you ran to the clubhouse. Ghosted me. Out of sight, out of mind. I thought I meant more to you than that."

There's one thing I've always known about Lindsey —she calls it like she sees it. And, as usual, she's not wrong. The clubhouse is my safe haven, and a part of me did run here. It was a selfish thing to do. Seeing the hurt on her face now tells me exactly how stupid I've been. Leaving her was the biggest mistake I've ever made.

"I know you blame me for the baby." Her chest heaves as a sob escapes her lips. "I see it in your eyes every time you look at me." A fat tear slips silently down her cheek as I gape at her, unable to believe what she just said.

"That's not fucking true," is all I can get out before my throat closes completely.

"I tried so hard," she sobs. "I prayed the baby would be okay, but I couldn't... There was nothing I could do."

"I know, baby," I say softly, moving toward her. I just want to wrap my arms around her and erase those terrible thoughts from her mind. "I know."

"How could you know?" she snaps, her face hard now. "You were in surgery, barely hanging on. You weren't there when the doctor came in to tell me what had happened. To tell me that our child was gone. When I told you..." Her breath shudders. "God, your face. It was like the doctor telling me all over again. I failed you and our baby."

"You didn't fail us, Lindsey. We failed each other. I should've never let you leave the clubhouse that night. I knew Tucker was after the kids, and I let you come out of lockdown to go with me. If I'd done what Judge had told me to do, we'd all be okay."

"Just stop. It's not okay. Nothing about this is okay." She starts to crumble, and I rush to her, pulling her tight against my chest. She sobs long and hard, her tears soaking through my shirt, but I don't give a shit. Holding her while she unravels is all that matters.

"Do you even still love me?" Her quiet question is muffled by my chest, but I can hear the fear in her words.

"More than anything, Lindsey." I dip my hand down to pull her chin up. "You're it for me, baby. End game. You have been since you started hiking that little skirt of yours up and parading around the clubhouse."

She chuckles a little at that, and I press a kiss to her forehead.

"We aren't doing a good job of being there for each other, are we?"

"I'm sorry I cut you out like I did. It won't happen again. Ever."

"Me too," she agrees, snuggling a little closer. "What do we do now?"

"We go home, sugar. That's what we do."

Chapter 9

LINDSEY

I HATE HOSPITALS. The smell. The sounds. The shuffling of soft-soled shoes as nurses and orderlies move from one room to the next. I especially hate this hospital. It's the one where I'd lost my baby and nearly lost Karma.

"You okay?" Blair asks as we step inside the elevator. Grace and Shelby stand on the other side of me with concerned, motherly looks on their faces.

I press my lips together and nod. "It's just this place," I say, my voice low. "Bad memories."

Blair wraps her arm around my waist and rests her head on my shoulder, while Grace takes my hand in hers.

And this is why I love these women. I haven't known any of them for a particularly long period of time, but this is my family. These women are my sisters. No matter how much shit I go through, I can always count on them for support, maybe a cold drink, and a sympathetic ear.

"We don't have to stay here," Shelby says, just as the elevator door opens to the fourth floor. "I can come back and see Marie tonight. It'll give Mom a chance to go home and get a shower."

Shaking my head, I draw in a deep breath before stepping out into the hallway.

"I'm fine. Besides, Marie needs us right now. And I could use something to focus on besides that."

Shelby nods, and Blair leads us to a sign pointing us toward the unit Mom's wife had been admitted to a couple of days ago. It had come as a shock to all of us when Marie's cancer had come back, but not nearly as much as it had Mom. Marie may have had her moments, but Mom has loved her through every one of them. Her prognosis is grim, and I'd overheard Judge telling Hashtag he wasn't sure Mom would ever get over it.

"What kind of name is Mom, anyway?" Blair asks. "He's the least feminine of them all, especially with that scar on his lip. You'd think his name would be Beast or Tank, or Griz... or something like that."

"Those names are for pussies," Mom growls from behind us.

Blair lets out a yelp and whirls around. We'd walked right by Marie's room.

"Moms are badasses. They call me Mom because

none of those fuckers can wipe their own ass without asking for help. I help every one of them handle the shit in their lives, and make sure that at the end of the day, all of them are good. That's about as Mom-like as it gets in an MC."

I grin and lean in, wrapping my arms around Mom's neck. He's been in the Black Hoods MC longer than I've been alive. He's like an uncle to me, and Marie's kind of like a crazy aunt a few fries short of a Happy Meal.

"How's she doing?" I ask.

Mom sighs and takes a step back. "Okay for now. They're keeping her comfortable, but there's nothing else to be done. Chemo isn't going to help. It's spread too far."

My belly does a swan dive as I look past him into Marie's room. From this angle, all I can see is her blanket covered toes. I can't imagine what either one of them is feeling right now.

Reaching for Mom's hand, I squeeze it. "I'm sorry, honey. How's she handling the news?"

He scoffs. "She ain't even worried. All she cares about is who's gonna wash my drawers once she's gone."

I smile. "She loves you."

Mom nods.

Silence hangs in the air until Blair utters, "You look whipped. Why don't you go home and take a shower, have a nap, get something to eat? We'll keep Marie company while you're gone."

Mom's gaze shifts as he looks at each one of us, almost assessing us.

"We won't get her too excited," Grace assures him.

Mom chuckles. "Honey, I'm more worried about her convincing you ladies to bust her outta here than anything."

"I will not," Marie calls from the room. *God, she sounds terrible.* Her voice is so weak and hoarse. It doesn't even sound like her. "Let them in, ya crusty old bastard."

All of us have a good giggle at that, but Mom rolls his eyes and leads us into the room. Marie's sitting up in the bed, her hair covered with a bright pink beanie. Her skin is washed out, and I swear I can see every vein in her body.

"Go home," she tells him. "Give me some time with the girls. You need a shower. Ya stink."

He leans over and kisses her on the forehead, telling her in a firm tone, "Behave."

"Never," she replies, grinning up at him.

Mom smiles and turns to the rest of us. "She causes you any trouble, call me."

"Go," Marie orders him, drawing out the word until he starts moving out of the room. Once he's gone, she flops back on the pillows and sighs. "Jesus Christ, I never thought he'd leave. I love that man to death, but he's smothering me here."

The other girls chuckle, and I move to sit on the edge of her bed. "How you doing in here, honey?"

"It's like prison," she whispers, raising her left hand and pointing at her IV. "But they have really good drugs, so I don't bother trying to bust out. Not yet, at least."

That statement is good for about thirty seconds of giggles, and then everyone goes quiet.

What do you say to a woman who knows she's dying? It's not like you can say much to reassure her. You can't exactly make the fear of death disappear.

"Oh, come on," Marie groans. "I'm not in the morgue yet, ladies. Sit. Talk."

Everyone does as they're told, finding different places to plant their behinds, while Marie turns her attention to me.

"You getting along with that old man of yours now?"

"We're here for you, Marie. Not to talk about my love life."

Marie gives my shoulder a gentle—and very weak—shove. "Fuck that. Your love life is far more exciting than me dying. Give me the tea, bitch."

And that's why Marie is Marie. She's a little nutty, but totally lovely.

"There's not much to talk about," I say, hoping we

can get off this topic and onto something a whole lot less... personal.

"Bullshit," Shelby huffs. "We all heard you and Karma fighting the other day."

"Yeah," Grace chimes in. "And we all heard what sounded like the opposite of fighting right after that."

The girls all have a good laugh, and my cheeks are probably glowing with embarrassment. They feel like they're on fire.

"You know how it is," I tell them. "Karma and I don't always get along, but we always find our way back to each other."

"That's called passion, honey," Marie insists. "And it's a rare find, so hold on to it and never let it go."

Pressing my lips together in a tight smile, I take her hand in mine. "I won't."

Tears form in Marie's eyes as she holds my gaze, but she's not someone who would ever let you see her cry. Instead, she blinks, shakes her head, and sighs loudly.

"Next topic. Grace, you pull that stick outta your ass yet?"

Grace's jaw drops, her mouth open in a stunned O, but I'm not sure any of us are looking any different.

Marie's head swivels as she takes in Grace, Lindsey, Shelby, and me, before throwing her hands up in the air, letting out the loudest, most infectious laugh I've ever heard. And that's when the rest of us can't take it another moment and join in with her.

Chapter 10

KARMA

"WOULD you stop fucking crunching back there? I can't hear myself think," I grouse, glaring back at Hashtag in the rearview mirror. With a snarky look, he pulls another chip from the bag and crunches it even louder. *Fucker.*

GP laughs in the passenger seat next to me. Twelve hours in this van, staring at the same garage from the woods across the street, is pushing my limit of annoyance. Between Hash and his chips, and my sore muscles battling against the worn seat of our borrowed work van, I'm about to fucking snap.

"Ya think?" Hashtag quips, shoving another chip into his mouth.

GP gives him a death glare. "Shut the fuck up, Hash."

He goes back to his chips, crunching away as if he

doesn't know how much it's grinding on my nerves, or just doesn't care.

"Think they'll show up?"

After more than two weeks of nothing, Hashtag had finally found a pattern between the break-ins, which involved a new parts shipment that would come in during the weekend. Trucks would show up on Saturday afternoon, and by Monday, the shop would be cleaned out lock, stock, and barrel. Judge had a theory about who was tipping off the guys, but the only way to find out was to see if they'd hit. So we had deliveries scheduled at all the old guys' shops and ours, with team's watching each of them. I apparently got the short end of the stick when I got Hashtag as my partner.

"If they do, they'll hear your ass before they even get out of their vehicle."

Hashtag reaches into the bag, but instead of pulling out another chip, he pulls out his middle finger and waves it in my direction.

I narrow my eyes. "Stow it or I'll break it off, asshat."

"Love to see you try."

Test me one more time, asshole. One more fucking time. I may be on the injured list, but I'll be damned if that'll stop me from whipping his ass.

"How did you get Judge to agree to let you come on our little garage sleepover, anyway?" GP asks, likely in an effort to stop the current conversation. "Thought you were still rehabbing it?"

"I am."

Rehab. The fucking pointless appointments that Lindsey forces me to attend. Lift this. Pull that. Focus on your breathing. It's all bullshit.

Getting back to work is the only thing that's going to rehabilitate me. At Lindsey's insistence, backed by Judge on the promise I'd be included in club shit, is the only reason I bother dragging my ass there every other day. Helga, my therapist, sure isn't the reason. She's a mean old lady who doesn't let up even a little when I grimace in pain or want to quit. If Judge wasn't shacked up with Grace, I'd be pushing her in front of him. She's just as bull-headed as he is.

"And that means your fit for duty how?"

"We need all hands on deck," I snap.

With Mom's old lady in the hospital, and whatever the fuck's going on with Stone Face, we were already spread a little thin. And with four shops to watch, we're doing the best we can. Prospects were called up, and we even had one of the sister chapters on standby to hit the road if shit went south.

My phone vibrates in my pocket, pulling it out I see a text with Lindsey's name pop up on the screen.

You doing okay?

I type out a quick response.

I'm good. You okay?

Three little dots pop up as she replies.

Good. I'm with the girls. Be careful out there tonight. Love you.

After all the shit we'd been through, and now me being back in the saddle part-time, Lindsey had given me a Judge style ultimatum about communication. If I couldn't call, I had to text. Did I like this level of babysitting? Fuck no. But if it keeps my balls out of the meat grinder and Lindsey happy, so I'll do it for now. I go to reply back when a pair of headlights swoops down the lane toward the shop.

"Showtime," GP mutters under his breath, pulling his side piece out of his holster. We all watch in silence as a large, black, unmarked truck pulls up to the front entrance of the shop. No one moves for over twenty minutes. Not us. Not the driver. No one. We watch and wait, and so do they.

With the click of a door opening, a man appears, being careful to stay deep in the shadows.

He has a large frame and is all decked out in black from head to toe. We watch in silence as he steps away from the vehicle on the driver's side. If it hadn't been for the noise of the door opening, we may not have noticed he was there at all. He lingers, watching and waiting before approaching the garage from the side entrance.

"Come on, fucker. Trigger the camera," Hashtag whispers.

The man flattens himself against the side of the building, inching his way toward the door.

"Got anything? GP asks.

When Hashtag's phone vibrates, he pulls up a moving image from the night vision camera.

"Got him. He's going in the side entrance."

A soft shattering of glass echoes through the still air.

"Any movement on the truck?"

GP swipes his finger across the screen, pulling up another camera. "Nothing."

"He's alone?" I muse. "One guy's doing this shit?"

"Looks that way. Ready, Hash?"

"Let's do it," he replies, shoving his phone in my hand.

"What the fuck am I supposed to do with this?"

"Watch it."

"The fuck I am. That's your job."

"Not tonight. I get to have the fun while you do the techie shit." The bastard has the balls to pat me on the shoulder. "Ironic, huh?"

"You ladies don't stop hen-pecking each other, we're all gonna be watching him get away," GP growls.

I allow my complaint to fall silent as he quietly opens the passenger door and climbs out. Without another word, Hashtag slips between the seats, following after him. GP stops, turns on his heel, and points a finger at me in warning.

"Stay in the fucking van."

I pause, gripping the door handle. "Fuck you, man."

"Judge's orders."

I watch from my seat as the duo creeps across the road, using the same shadows as the fucker looting the garage to sneak up to the building. Hashtag stops at the edge and looks back at me, shooting me the bird as he disappears into the darkness. *Motherfucker.* It's all fun and games while I'm still recovering, but the first ass I'm going to kick is his. Might even do it twice.

My heart thuds in my chest. This is my job, not theirs. Shame and anger course through my veins. I should be out there with them, protecting their six. Not sitting in the fucking van watching this stupid phone.

I swipe over to the tab that shows me inside. Nothing moves. GP slips inside the door first, going right, while Hashtag goes left, guns at the ready. A shout and repeated gunfire draws my attention away from the phone and to the door. The camera isn't showing me a goddamn thing. My brothers are in there.

"Fuck this shit." Throwing open the door, I bolt for the building. Pain shoots across my chest, and by the time I reach the door, I feel like I've run a marathon and not just across the road. My breathing is rapid and shaky by the time I find both Hashtag and GP struggling with the biggest motherfucker I've ever seen. He swings his left arm wide, knocking Hashtag back. This is about to go south fast.

Rushing over, I rear my leg back and deliver a solid kick to the man's temple with my boot. Going limp, he drops to the floor in a pile of black clothing.

Hashtag gapes at me, his arms thrown out wide. "The fuck you think you're doing, K?"

"Saving your asses. You're welcome, by the way."

"I had him," GP growls.

"Didn't look that way to me." I shrug, pretending my heart isn't racing like a fucking stampede inside of my chest. Therapy is just short bursts of activity, so this is the hardest I've pushed myself since the shooting. I lean back against a toolbox when Hashtag gets to his feet, pushing past me.

"He still breathing?"

"Yeah," GP replies. "Lucky for him, you're not at full strength. A kick like that should've killed him."

"Help me get him up." Hash takes one of his arms, and between the two of them, they jerk the man to his feet. He has to be at least three hundred pounds of solid muscle. With him as dead weight, getting him outside won't be easy.

"Fucker's heavier than he looks," Hash hisses through gritted teeth.

"Hang on." Spotting something that'll help, I walk

over to a vehicle sitting on the lift and find a hand cart. Wheeling it through to the other side of the shop, I park it next to them. "This should do it."

GP eyes it. "Is that a fucking cart? It would be easier if you just gave us a hand here."

"I'm supposed to stay in the van, asshole. Remember?"

"Yeah, I remember."

They load him on with his feet placed firmly at the bottom of the cart. It takes a few minutes to restrain and stabilize him, thanks to a pair of straps I manage to find on a nearby tool bench. GP and Hashtag shove into the back of it to get it moving, making it out the door with a little extra effort. I try to secure the door as best I can while they deal with him. It's not the best patch job, but the likelihood of someone coming back tonight to look for him is slim.

Pulling my phone from my pocket, I shoot off a quick text to Judge, letting him know we got one of the guys.

Bring him to the clubhouse.

"Judge wants him brought back."

"You know," Hashtag huffs between shoves, "they make this look so much easier in the movies."

It takes them a few minutes to dump his ass into the back of the van, right on his face. If he wasn't knocked out before, he sure as fuck is now. Chuckling, I slam the door closed when they're finished.

"What do you want to do about the truck?"

"You take it."

"They could be tracking it," Hashtag notes. "We could lead them right back to the clubhouse if we take it with us."

He has a point. We don't need these guys hauling ass to our place.

"What do you think we should do?"

"I'll check for a GPS tracker and pull the data if I can, then we ditch it."

"Sounds like a plan," GP adds. "How long do you need?"

"Five minutes."

"Do it."

Hashtag jogs off toward the truck, leaving GP glaring at me.

"You good?"

"Fine."

"Bullshit, man. We had it back there. You could've gotten yourself hurt with that cowboy shit you pulled."

"Did the job, didn't it?"

"Yeah, but at what cost if it had gone wrong? It's not just you anymore, man. You need to remember that."

Is he right? Maybe. But I needed this. I need this club. Without it, what the fuck is my purpose? Sidelined or not, none of my brothers will go into a fight alone. Not a damn one.

LINDSEY

"YOU MEAN I PASSED?" I stare at Professor McCallen, unsure if I should squeal like a schoolgirl and hop across her mahogany desk to hug her, or play it cool, like the professional university graduate I'm about to be.

"I had no doubt you would," she replies with a rare smile. "You're a bright young woman, Lindsey. You have the ability to go very far in our field." She leans forward. "So make sure to cultivate your knowledge at every opportunity. Don't squander it."

I can't stop smiling. "Oh, I won't."

She chuckles. "You're all set to graduate with your class on Friday. I've given the go ahead to the committee."

"Thank you," I say, my voice breathless and full of gratitude.

"No thanks necessary, Miss Sheridan. This has all been on your own merit. Even the trauma you've recently been through hasn't had much of an effect on your studies. You're going to be a remarkable psychologist."

I wish I could keep my emotions in check, but when the heat hits my cheeks, I know Professor McCallen is getting a head-on view of my self-consciousness.

"That said," she continues, "I don't normally do this for my students, but a friend of mine has been working closely with a prestigious center in Houston, and she told me of a staff psychologist position that has recently become available. I instantly thought of you."

I blink back at her. "I..." I have no words. On one hand, this is huge. If Professor McCallen is recommending the job, then it must be good. But on the other hand, it's in Houston, and my life is here, in Austin.

Reaching into her desk, she pulls out a business card and hands it to me. "There's no pressure," she assures me. "But it's a wonderful opportunity the likes of which most of your fellow graduates won't come across for several years. Excellent pay, a gorgeous office, and even a furnished condo, on-site."

I stare down at the card. It almost sounds too good to be true. "Sounds wonderful," I admit.

Professor McCallen simply nods and gets to her feet. "The number is on the card. If you want to learn more about the position, simply give them a call. The job is yours if you want it."

I blink again. "Thank you."

I bid the professor farewell, likely for the last time before I graduate, and make my way out to the parking lot, never taking my eyes off the card in my hand. The Houston Health Institute.

Fancy.

Just then, my phone rings. It takes me a second to snap out of my trance and dig in my purse for it. Karma.

"Hey, baby," I say in greeting. Reaching my car, I climb inside and close the door. "Guess what."

"What?"

"I get to graduate with my class!"

He sounds pleased. "Yeah?"

I nod, as if he can see me. "Yep. This time next week, you'll be fucking a PhD."

He chuckles. "Now that's the sexiest thing I've heard all day."

"Right?" I tease. "So what's up?"

"Well…" He drags out the word, and I know instantly that his news isn't going to be good. "I have to stay late tonight. We have some shit to work out here."

I frown. "What do you mean, we? Are you back to doing club shit already? 'Cause Judge agreed that until the doctor gives you the go ahead—"

"It's fine," he snaps. "Enough. Jesus Christ. I'm so

sick and fucking tired of everyone talking about this. I'm fine. I'm taking it easy, but I'm not going to just sit around on my ass anymore. The club's going to shit, and I'm going to do my part, okay?"

"No," is all I say, even though I can think of other words to say instead. One in particular comes to mind, and it has four letters.

"Too bad," he snarls. "I'll be home, but it'll be late. Don't wait up."

The call disconnects before I can even think of my reply.

Dropping the phone onto the passenger seat, I grit my teeth and slam my fist against the steering wheel. Fucking Karma. I just don't get him anymore.

I'd lived with Uncle Judge for years as a young girl. I had to make my own meals and get a ride to school with friends more than I liked, but he always came home at night, and always gave me his time.

Not Karma, though. Lately, I've been learning he doesn't much care about my time at all. He cares about himself. I'm surprised he even bothered giving me a heads up at this point.

Maybe he'd care more if I was in Houston.

Just as fast as the thought floats through my mind, I jam it down deep. No, I could never leave my family. And as much as he pisses me off—especially lately—I could never leave Karma.

No. Houston isn't even an option, but a chat with Uncle Judge about helping me sort Karma out is. If Karma won't slow down for me, he'll sure as hell slow down for his president. And I think at this point, it's the only option he's left me with.

Chapter 12

KARMA

"YOU'RE GOING to be late if you don't hurry up," I yell from outside the ladies' restroom. She'd spent a few hours at home with Blair, trying on dresses and doing their girlie shit before I had to drag them both out of the house.

She steps out of the bathroom for the what seems like the fifth time at the assembly hall. Her body is cloaked in a graduation gown, with a tight black dress underneath that makes me think about all the ways I want to peel it off of her later.

You can't even fuck her right. Why do you think she'd want you?

The memory of our failed attempts over the last few days nag at me. It takes effort, but I shove them down and try not to focus on the few pairs of eyes that drift her way. She could have any of these educated bastards, yet she's here with me.

As soon as she gets close, she looks down at her feet.

"Do I look okay?" she asks again.

"Gorgeous," I say with a smile, hoping it doesn't look as phony as it feels. "Nervous?"

She shrugs. "I guess so. It doesn't seem real that I'm actually getting my degree."

Pulling her close, I wrap my arms around her. "You put in the work, baby. You deserve this." I want to tell her how proud I am that she's gone from an abandoned teenager living with an MC to a Doctor of Psychology, but the words won't come out of my mouth. She's accomplished so much, and as much as I've tried to support her, I almost cost her this graduation. Me and my shit made her fail that fucking test. If her professor hadn't taken pity on her, we wouldn't be standing here now.

"Students!" a man in a hat who looks to be straight out of some period drama television show calls out to the room. "Please get in line for the procession."

Her face turns back to me as her body stiffens.

"You'll do great, babe," I assure her.

"I worry I'm going to fall on my face."

"So what if you do? I'll be there to catch you."

She playfully smacks my chest. "Yeah, right. You're going to run up on that stage to catch me in your condition?" I frown, and she takes notice. "That's not what I meant. I'm sorry."

Pretending to feign indifference, I force a smile against her painful reminder. "I didn't hear shit. Go get in line and get that degree." Lies. All fucking lies. Her words are like a barb straight to my heart. I can't let her see it, or she won't leave me. These last few months have been all about me, and today has to be about her.

"You sure?" she questions, watching my face for any indication that I'm not okay.

"Get your ass in that line, woman."

Pulling away, she heads toward the line of students outside the auditorium doors. She looks back and waves before she disappears inside, but I don't budge. The hallway is where I belong. Not in there with her family after I nearly cost her graduating. My taint needs to stay away from her until that degree is in her hand. Grace, Judge, and Blair have all that covered for me.

Time ticks by slowly. Name after name gets called out, and my body stiffens when I hear hers. I know she's looking out in that crowd for me, smiling for me, and I'm not even in there. The school's band strikes up a song, and the doors open with the procession of the students following them. Lindsey's beautiful face pops through the doorway, and when she zeroes in on me, she stalks over with that degree tucked in her hands.

"Where the hell were you?" she snarls, anger lacing

every syllable. "Why weren't you sitting with the rest of them?"

She did notice. *Fuck. Here we go.*

"Too crowded," I lie.

When she opens her mouth to say something, Blair screams her name.

"Congratulations, Lins!" she cries, pulling her into a tight hug. "I'm so proud of you."

Blair steps aside, letting Grace take her place. Judge and I stand back, allowing the ladies to do their thing.

"You got a reason for missing this moment in her life?" he mutters under his breath.

"I do."

"Better be a good fucking reason, son, because milestones like this? You don't miss those for the people you love."

He steps away and walks up to Lindsey, beaming with pride. I observe just how happy she is with her family around her. The family that she chose. The family I wanted for us but will never have. There won't be moments like this for us and our kids. No graduations. No weddings. No birthday parties.

The proud party wagon breaks away and they all turn to me.

"Ready to go?" I force out with a smile.

"Go where?"

"Did you think we weren't going to celebrate?" Blair chirps.

"You didn't." Lindsey gasps, gazing at me.

"Oh, we did," Grace chimes in. "Cake, balloons—the whole nine yards."

Lindsey's fake smile is good enough to fool them, but not me. She didn't want a party. She just wanted a quiet celebration, but as soon as Blair and Grace got wind of that, they blew it all out of proportion. If she wasn't pissed already, she will be now.

We head out of the building together, everyone talking around us, but neither of us says a word. Everyone shuffles away to their own rides except for Blair, who rode with us to the ceremony. She and Lindsey chatter all the way to the clubhouse. I can almost feel the frustration radiating off of Lindsey when she takes note of all the cars parked outside.

"Hope you're ready for a big night," Blair exclaims giddily as she hops out of the car. "Give me five minutes before you come in. I need to make sure GP didn't mess up my instructions."

She closes the door behind her, leaving us in silence. Lindsey shifts in her seat to look at me.

"This isn't what I wanted."

"I know, Lins, but you know Blair. She wanted a party. And when she got Grace involved, it went off the fucking rails."

"You could've stopped them."

She's right. I could have, but I didn't. I let them take over the one aspect she asked me to handle because I knew I would fuck it up. Turns out, I fucked up worrying about fucking up.

"You didn't even watch me walk across the stage to get this." She waves the black leather diploma holder in my face. "I don't know why I even expected you to follow through on this. I should've just gone on my own."

"I'm sorry, Lindsey, I am. I just—"

"Stop with the excuses." Her tone comes out more as a demand this time. "I thought we were past this, Karma. Things have been going so well, but I guess I shouldn't expect things to change when only one of us is putting in the work."

"Hold the fuck on," I growl. "I've been putting in the work. I text when I'm gone. I come home every night. I came to your fucking ceremony. What more do you want from me?"

"I want you to be the man you used to be. The one who loved me. The one who was there for me. Not a fucking ghost."

Jumping out, she slams the door closed, leaving me to watch her walk away, heading straight for the building. Once she's at the door, she stops, looks back at me from over her shoulder, and wipes away her tears before stepping inside.

I punch the steering wheel, and the recoil sends a jolt of pain through my arm. Fucking stupid. I had one job today, making sure she was happy, and I fucking failed at that. She's as miserable as I am. Just what I fucking needed today.

A fist slams against my window. Hashtag, wearing his goofy ass grin, stands outside my truck and shouts, "Party's inside, jackass! You comin', or are you gonna sit out here all night?"

I pop open the door, nudging him with it, and slide out, slamming it behind me.

"Someone's in a mood today," he remarks. "It's a party, man. Where's your happy face?"

"How about I deck you, and we see if we find it there?"

Shaking his head, he trudges off and heads inside. Following behind him, I hesitate as I reach for the door. If I go in there, it'll just make it worse. And if I don't, same fucking thing. Damned if I do, damned if I don't. Pulling open the door, I take my chances with the only outcome there is.

The main room of the clubhouse has colored streamers everywhere. Balloons billow from the center of card tables set up around the room. My brothers, their old ladies, and their kids litter the room. Kevin and Natalie, along with Hashtag's daughter Hayden, are dancing to the music from the Bluetooth sound system off in the corner. It's good to see that they're at least having a good time.

I spot Lindsey nestled up next to the bar with GP and Blair. Taking a deep breath, I head off to their group.

Blair smiles when she sees me. "I wondered where you went off to."

"I was outside, taking a breather," I lie.

"Beer?" GP offers, grabbing one from a metal container filled with ice from the bar top.

"Fuck yeah, man." Grabbing it from his hand, I twist off the cap and chug it back. "Hit me again."

GP eyes me before reaching back and grabbing another one. "You good, man?"

"I will be when you give me that fucking brew."

Lindsey stills next to me. "But the doctor said…"

"Don't see them here. It's a party, isn't it?" Snatching the bottle from GP, I take a leisurely swig. "Why aren't you drinking, sugar? It's your party."

"Someone has to be sober enough to drive us home," she smarts back.

"Drink, Lins. I can drive you home."

Lindsey shifts her gaze over to Blair. I don't think I've ever seen Blair without a drink in her hand at any of our parties.

"That's weird," Lindsey muses. "What's up with that?"

"It's your night. I wanted to make sure you had a way home."

"Bullshit," Lindsey fires back. "You're hiding something."

Blair blushes. "I'm not. This is your party, and I just want you to have a good time." She tries to laugh it off, but Lindsey keeps on it like a bloodhound.

"Drop it, Lins," I warn her. "Whatever it is, Blair doesn't want to talk about it."

"Stay out of this," she growls at me before starting back in on Blair. "Why wouldn't I have a good time if you're drinking?"

"Please, Lindsey."

"Please what, Blair?"

"It's not the right time."

"Right time for what?"

"Why don't you and I go dance, Red?" GP interjects, trying to pull her out of the conversation. What the hell has GP wanting to run?

"You're fucking pregnant, aren't you?" GP's body goes rigid.

Oh, fuck, not tonight. Fuck.

"I didn't want you to find out this way," Blair tears up as the words leave her lips. "I wanted to wait until you had a little more time."

Lindsey grows eerily quiet next to me.

"I'm sorry, Lins. Please talk to me."

Stepping in, I pull Lindsey close. She looks up at me, tears welling in her eyes. "I…" she splutters before I cut her off.

"We're happy for you both. It'll be nice to have some kids around here."

The last syllable barely makes it into the conversation before Lindsey shoves away from my grasp and runs toward the exit, with Blair hot on her heels, leaving me standing here like an idiot.

"Fuck!" I exclaim, slamming my beer down on the bar top.

"You okay, man?"

"No," I growl. "This whole day has been fucked from the start, and I just fucked it even more."

"Shouldn't you go after her?"

"I'm the last person she wants to see right now, GP."

He frowns. "You sure about that? This can't be easy news for her, considering what the two of you went through not all that long ago."

"Yeah, I am. Going after her is the last thing she wants."

Chapter 13

LINDSEY

"I DON'T LIKE THIS," Uncle Judge grunts, slamming the lid down on the trunk of my car. "You're going to break him."

I look at him, my heart filled with more sadness than I ever remember feeling in my life. "He's already broken. I think we both are."

"This won't help."

"I can't fix him. I'm only making things worse."

We both are. I've tried getting him to open up more to me, but he just shuts me down. He's stuck in a spiral of depression and self-loathing. Every single textbook method I've tried has yet to work. This is the only option for the both of us if we ever want to be happy again. The old adage of if you love something, set it free.

Uncle Judge sighs and pulls me into his arms, resting his chin on top of my head. "Oh, honey. You guys have had tragedy written all over you since the day this thing started. This isn't the life I wanted for you after what your mom did."

He sounds as sad as I feel.

"I need this, Uncle Judge," I assure him, pulling back to meet his gaze. "I feel like I've lost absolutely everything, like there's no hope. But I also know that's not true. I need to reshape the way I do things, refigure the expectations I've set out for myself and for whoever I end up with in the future."

He nods. "You're a smart woman, Lins. And trust me, I understand. You've been through more at your age than anyone should have to. Now you've got the means to turn that shit around. Go. Live. And most importantly, be fucking happy."

Happy. That word doesn't even want to fit into my personal vocabulary lately. Right now, I'm just living to survive. That's my only goal—to survive. And maybe along the way, I'll find a new normal, and the way back to myself again.

"You have to promise me you'll keep an eye on him."

"Always do, honey. He's going to want to know where you went. I'll be the first person he comes to when he realizes you're gone."

"You can't tell him where I've gone. Coming after me is not an option."

"You're gonna drive him mad. You know that, right?"

He takes a step back and rakes a hand through his graying hair. "You guys may be having major issues, but he loves you. Not knowing where you're at is going to drive him over the edge."

I consider that. In a way, it almost serves him right. I mean, it's not like he ever tells me where he is anymore.

"Tell him I'm safe, but no more than that."

He takes a moment to respond. "If that's what you want, consider it done."

Popping up on my toes, I press a kiss to his bearded cheek. "Kiss the kids for me."

"Behave," is all he says in return.

It's the closest I'm going to get to an emotional good-bye, so I roll with it. Pulling back, I give him one last smile and climb in behind the wheel.

Starting it up, I shift into reverse. Before easing my foot off the brake, I take one last look at the house I've been sharing with Karma since he got home from the hospital. We hadn't lived here long, but part of it had felt like home. But it wasn't anymore. Now it's just Karma's home.

My home is in Houston, or it will be. My fresh start away from all of this.

With a final wave toward my uncle, I force a smile and back out of the driveway.

I try not to think of what Karma will go through when he notices I'm gone. But honestly, I don't even know when that'll be. It's been three days since my graduation, and I haven't seen or heard a word from him.

He's texted a few times, but I couldn't bring myself to reply. I guess maybe it's petty, but I consider it like payback for all the times he went dark on me. He hadn't come looking, though. Not even then. I could be dead in the house for all he knows, and I can't live that way anymore.

So I'd called the number Professor McCallen had given me and accepted the position of staff psychologist at the Houston Health Institute. And because he's too focused on himself, Karma remains none-the-wiser.

This job is what I need right now. A chance to escape. A chance to utilize what I've learned and really make a difference in people's lives. I can't do that here. Not now. Not with the way things have been.

I've been drowning. Not only in my own self-pity, but in Karma's too, and I can't sink down any lower. I'm pulling myself out of it by going to Houston. I'm going to give Karma the space he needs to save himself, all while saving myself in the process.

Chapter 14

KARMA

"JUST FUCKING GIVE us something about your boss, man," I growl.

"Fuck you," he hisses through gritted teeth, spraying blood from his busted lips. We've been at this for over a week now since picking up his big fucking ass from one of the garages. We'd let him sit and think about his next move during Lindsey's graduation party, but the last few days have been an onslaught of trying to make him talk. Watching my brothers do my fucking job while I was ordered to observe and advise by Judge.

"Do it," I order, nodding to Stone Face who had rolled back into the clubhouse yesterday morning without a damn explanation for where he's been. He cracks his big knuckles and rears back, landing a solid hit to the guy's gut. He winces and yells in pain. "Again."

Stone Face repeats his strike, this time aiming a little lower. Still fucking nothing.

The wooden door of the shed pulls open, and the morning light peeks through when Judge slips inside, taking in the man's mangled face and blood spatter. Stone Face continues with his beatdown, landing hit after hit, like he's in the middle of the Octagon fighting the guy who talked shit about his mama. He switches his hit location and aims right for his kidneys. Seconds later, the guy slumps back into a heap, unconscious.

"Enough," Judge barks. "He's out." Stone's broad chest heaves when his fists finally fall to his sides. "Take a break, brother."

Stone Face trudges past us, leaving Judge and I alone with our sleeping friend.

"Anything?" he inquires, sidling up next to me.

"Not a fucking thing. Fucker's like Fort Knox. Not a damn peep. Hash find anything?"

"He's got some leads, but I sent him home for a few hours. Found him passed out at his keyboard."

We were all getting there. Between the shit with these garages, and my fuck up with Lindsey's graduation party, I'm fucking beat down. Not that I would admit that to anyone here.

"What's the plan now? We got silent mouse here, and nothing concrete from the van. We're getting a whole lot of nowhere fast with this guy. I don't know how much longer he can hold on."

Judge pinches the bridge of his nose between his two large fingers. Frustration is getting the best of us. We've dealt with some rough shit before, but these thefts are bringing us all to our breaking points. Well, everyone but this fucker.

"No shit, K," he growls. "I was hoping he'd start singing."

"Judging by the way his jaw is busted up, I don't think he'll be saying much. We've only got one choice."

Judge knows I'm right. Silent mouse here isn't going to give us shit. We need to cut our losses and hope Hash's info pans out.

"Do it," Judge orders. "I'll get V and Priest to clean up the mess."

Nodding in response, I pull out my sidepiece, pulling back the hammer as I approach him. The man is still out, and it's better this way with what's coming. Murder or mercy, I'm sparing him from the fate the people pulling his strings would have in store for him if we released him. Aiming for his head, I fire without looking away. One clean shot through and through, the mess spraying against the back wall of the shed.

Picking up my brass, I stuff it in my pocket and slide my handgun back into the holster on my hip. "Prospects have their work cut out for them. Should just burn the fucking shed down."

"They'll figure it out."

"What do you want me to do now, Prez?"

"Go home," he replies with a slight hesitation in his voice. I arch my brow, and he realizes I caught that. "Been a long couple of days for all of us."

Shaking off the weirdness, I follow Judge out of the shed. He barks out orders to V and Priest who are sitting outside the back entrance of the clubhouse, neither one looking particularly happy to have to clean up my mess.

Stopping, Judge turns to me before heading inside. "Let me know when you get home."

"Yeah, sure thing," I reply suspiciously.

The fuck? He's normally not this concerned. I'm tired, but not too tired to drive my own ass the couple of miles to the house. Worst case, I'd crash here for a few hours since Lindsey's still giving me the silent treatment after the shitstorm at the graduation party. Apparently, her little communication rule only applies to me and not her.

Pulling out my phone, I fire off another text to Lindsey, letting her know I'm heading home. It beeps a few seconds later with an undeliverable message. Fucking great. She's turned off her phone again to ignore me. Any chances of getting some shut-eye just went out the window, knowing the fight waiting at home for me.

I walk around the clubhouse and head for my truck.

Judge comes out the front door with Stone Face and Mom in tow as I climb inside, all looking at me. No wave. No middle fingers. Maybe it's the exhaustion, but something doesn't feel right. Shaking it off, I head for home.

During the drive, I think about what I'm going to tell Lindsey. How I am going to apologize for what I said and did on her graduation day? I royally fucked up. And then dealing with our now permanently silent friend, she's had way too much time to stew on it. She'll be a lit powder keg to my match, my presence at home igniting the explosion between us.

Her car isn't there when I pull into the drive. I look at the time on the radio of my truck. Seven in the morning. Even when she was in grad school, she was never up and out of the house before ten.

Pulling out my phone, I bark into the receiver, "Call Lindsey."

"Calling Lindsey," it replies back before connecting the call. I frown when I hear an automated voice tell me, "The number you're trying to reach is not in service."

The fuck it isn't. I pay the goddamn bill. I try calling her a second time, only to get the same recording.

She's pissed at me. She's probably blocked my number and is staying at Blair's.

I bolt from the truck, not bothering to close the door.

With long strides, I make it to the front porch, my hands a blur as I turn the lock.

"Lindsey?" I call out into the quiet house. I walk into the living room. Nothing. I move on to the kitchen. She's not there. Pulling out my phone, I dial Blair's number. It rings and rings.

"Pick up. Pick Up… Fuck!" I roar.

I search the house, every fucking inch of it, but it's when I make it to the bedroom that the realization hits me. The double closet I'd had remodeled for her lies open and empty. Her shoe collection's gone. The fucking stuffed animal I won for her at a carnival years ago is gone.

She's gone. *She left me*.

"No. No. No!" I yell, dragging my hands through my hair. This can't be happening. Backing up, I run into the bed and fall back against it. I see a photo of the two of us on my nightstand, and it fills me with rage. Picking it up, I slam it against the wall, watching the glass shatter, just like my heart.

My phone rings in my clutched fist. Peering down at it, I see Judge's name on the screen.

"Where the fuck is she?" I scream into the phone. "Where the fuck is Lindsey?"

"She's gone, Karma."

"Tell me where she is, old man."

"I don't know where she is. Just know that she's

safe."

"She's not fucking safe. She's not here with me."

"Son, this is for the best, for both of you. You've both been through some shit, and you need to work it out on your own."

"Stay the fuck out of my business, Judge. You don't know shit." Anger reverberates throughout my entire body. Work shit out? We were doing that until this. We were never going to be the perfect couple, but fuck, I thought she at least still wanted to try.

"I know everything I need to know. You two are at each other's throats, suffering because neither one of you can handle what happened. She needs this just as much as you do."

No. I need *her*. I need her here with me, where I can protect her, and not worry about where she is or who she's with. *Fuck. Don't even think about that shit.*

"Go fuck yourself."

"You're doing a good enough job of that all on your own. Your anger and resentment is getting the best of you. It's high time you stop being so damned angry and start working on yourself physically, and deal with whatever the fuck's going on in that head of yours. Until you can do that, you don't deserve her."

Deserve her? I never deserved her. She's always been out of my league, and now... she's out of my life.

LINDSEY

THE HOUSTON HEALTH INSTITUTE is luxury at its finest. Professor McCallen wasn't kidding when she said this position was an opportunity most wouldn't come across.

A health retreat for the wealthy, nestled at the edge of the city, right along the spectacular Lake Conroe. For the past few weeks, I've been working here as one of three staff psychologists under that friend Professor McCallen had mentioned, Dr. Gail Bardot.

I have an office that overlooks an immaculately groomed courtyard, bigger than the main floor of the house I'd shared with Karma. It came pre-decorated in beiges and browns, and an ivory that set the whole room off perfectly.

My condo is on site as well. Just a short walk away from the main resort, right along a pressure treated wooden boardwalk, was a building that housed fifteen staff condominiums. Mine just so happened to be on the ground floor. It had a sliding glass door that opened up and allowed me to sit on my patio, where I could stare out at the water and watch the sunset each night.

I love it here. Mostly.

Honestly, it's the perfect job. One many people work their entire careers to achieve, and I'd slid right into it as if it had been tailored to fit my needs. But there's no Karma. And there's no Twat Knot with his pervy jokes, or Stone Face with his grouchy glare. There's no Grace or Blair, and no Shelby.

It's lonely.

"So when Daddy said he wouldn't keep paying on my credit card, I didn't know what else to do," Vanessa Kingston sobs in the seat across from mine. "I mean, what kind of father does that? He just cut me off like I was nothing!"

Reaching for a box of tissues on the table beside me, I lean forward and offer them to her.

"I can imagine that was very difficult for you. It sounds like you felt abandoned by him."

Snatching a couple of tissues from the box, she gently pats around her eyes, though I don't see a single tear on her perfect skin.

"I did. And I didn't know what else to do, so I called Richard."

It takes great strength not to roll my eyes when I ask, "Richard is the older man you'd met when you were on vacation in Vale, correct?"

Vanessa nods, her blonde ponytail bouncing behind her. "He promised to take care of me. He told me he loved me."

I peek down at my watch to see it's nearly four o'clock, which means not only is it almost the end of this hellish session with Vanessa, but also the end of my day.

As much as I love this job, it's so hard to sit in a chair, day after day, and listen to rich men and women bitch and moan about stuff most of us could only imagine. Botched plastic surgeries, loss of their trust funds. Not getting invited to the socialite event of the year.

None of them would fit into my world, and it takes effort to appear to fit into theirs. Even still, I don't know if I'm doing it right.

After validating Vanessa's heartbreak for the hundredth time over an hour period, I bid her farewell and move to the desk to grab my purse. I have zero plans for the evening, but I'm looking forward to being in my own space, away from all the rich folks, surrounded only by the silence of the lake.

"Knock, knock."

I look up just in time to see Mr. Frost step into my office. Abe Frost is the President of the Houston Health Institute, and the man responsible for signing my paycheck. He also gives me the creeps. His eyes always seem to follow me whenever we're in the same room, and they're always on my face.

"Glad I caught you. I was hoping you and I could grab some dinner tonight."

He moves closer—far too close. His expensive suit jacket slides across my bare arm like silk, but instead of feeling sexy, it just feels wrong. And gross.

"Sorry, sir." I take a step back, trying to put some distance between us. "I have plans tonight."

He frowns, his wrinkled forehead wrinkling even deeper. "Oh? With who?"

I open my mouth to reply, but nothing comes out. I've always been a terrible liar, and this time, even though I'm only lying for self-preservation purposes, I still can't quite make it happen.

"With me." Both Frost and I look at Nora, leaning against the doorframe. Getting my attention, she motions for me to get a move on. "We have dinner plans in an hour. We better get moving."

She's lying. God bless her, she's lying way better than I ever could. Nora's been working as a psychologist here for a couple of years now, and she seems nice enough. And she's the only staff member who comes close to me in age.

"Right!" I chirp, ignoring Frost's suspicious gaze.

Like I said, I'm a terrible liar. "Was there anything else, Mr. Frost? I really do have to go."

His dark gaze darts between us before finally shaking his head. "No, that was it," he says, sounding more than a little disappointed. "You ladies enjoy your evening."

Placing the strap of my purse over my shoulder, I force a smile and nod. "You too, sir." With that, I shove past him and out of the room.

Nora doesn't say a word until we're halfway to the staff residences. "I'm sorry if I misread that. I just know the way he can be sometimes. You looked like you needed a quick out."

I chuckle. "Are you kidding? I owe you one."

"Actually, I'm heading out to the mall shortly. You want to come along? We can grab a drink at the pub on the way home."

I smile, happy for the first time in a while. "Absolutely. Lead the way."

Chapter 16

KARMA

"KEEP GOING," Helga snaps from behind me in her heavy accent. "Too slow."

The sound of blood pumping in my ears muffles the rest of her orders. My heart feels like it's about to explode inside my chest all over again. Each rotation of the stationary bike she's sidled me with today for my physical therapy appointment has been pure torture.

"Slow my ass," I mumble under my breath, but the glare she throws back at me tells me she heard it.

"Language!" she warns, glaring at me. When I start to lose momentum, she taps her knuckle on the timer at the top of the handlebars. "You still have ten more minutes, then we move to weights."

"You're trying to kill me," I pant between breaths.

"No," she corrects me. "I am trying to make you stronger."

Moving away from me, she checks in on an elderly man walking on a treadmill not far from my station. Freedom from her watchful eye. Week six of this shit routine, and I feel no better. My chest still burns when I exert myself in any way, and I can't catch my breath. The second I leave these sessions, I end up crashing for hours. Nothing is improving, which is why I never wanted to do this in the first place. It's a waste of time. Halfway through, and I'm no better than when I started.

Helga notices my sluggishness and stalks back over, her hands resting on her hips.

"I said don't stop. Don't you want to get better?"

The truth? I don't know. But for all intents and purposes, I give her the answer she wants to hear to get her off my case.

"Sure."

"That attitude is not helping you, Mr. Reed. You're behind on every single indicator to move on to the next phase. You need to pick up the pace, or we'll have to extend your program."

Like fuck that'll happen. I'm only here to appease Judge's demands. I do this shit, I get more of my club responsibilities back. Extending this ain't gonna happen.

"That's not my name. Call me Karma."

"Your paperwork says Evan Reed, and that's what I am going to call you. Not some silly nickname." Her hands move from her wide hips and come to rest over her large tits. "Start pedaling, Evan."

Evan Reed. The name I refuse to acknowledge unless the government fucking forces me to use it. The name that Lindsey liked to say when we were alone, like it was a secret between us.

Stop fucking thinking about her. She left. She's gone. Nothing I do will make her come back.

"Karma." It comes off in a clipped tone, filled with a menacing vibe.

"I don't know why I bother with you. No wonder that pretty girl doesn't come with you anymore."

"Don't talk about her." Clenching my jaw, my feet instantly stop moving. It's been four weeks since Lindsey bailed, and I've been trying really fucking hard not to think about her, or the destruction and void she left behind. *Lies. All fucking lies.* "Not another word about her."

Helga catches on quickly that she's crossed the line. Her arms fall from her chest, and she takes a few steps back, putting more distance between us.

"I–I didn't mean to—," she stammers. "I just wanted to motivate you to work harder."

"Enough." I slide off the stationary bike, my anger coiling like a viper preparing to strike at her on top of my already pounding heart. "I'm fucking done."

"Mr. Reed," she pleads when I stalk past her,

flinching when she realizes she just said that name again. Grabbing my cut and keys from the cubby, I charge through the gym entrance and past the receptionist. Her face freezes in fear when Helga comes after me, stopping only at the door because of the other patients in the room.

"Please, don't give up on this. My job is to push you, even when you believe you can't do it."

I don't acknowledge her words, letting her think they've fallen on deaf ears. She's no different from anyone else pushing me, reminding me every single day that Lindsey left me as a motivational tool to make me fix the shit going on in my head and with my own body. Not realizing that every time they say her name, it only fucks with me more.

I make it through the front door before the last drop of energy I have drains away. Bending over, I rest my hands on my knees as I suck in air, in and out, until the racing inside of my chest slows. Strangers stop to check on me, but I send them on their way with a glare. At least I still have that going for me.

Righting myself, I take labored steps until I make it to my truck. I unlock the door and slide inside, the silence roaring in my ears like a deafening storm. The one new constant in my life since she left. The reason why I've been sleeping at the clubhouse in my old room for weeks on end. My house is only a reminder of what I had with her.

Shoving the key into the ignition, I fire up the Hemi and peel out of the parking lot, heading straight for the clubhouse.

Pulling in, I take in all the bikes. Fucking great. The peanut gallery is here.

Climbing out of the truck, I head straight through the door and into the main room, finding the place empty except for Judge and Mom convening in the corner of the room, their heads close, their voices low. The longer I watch them, the more my anger slips away.

Judge clasps Mom's shoulder when his head drops. Shit. Something's up. I approach slowly, waiting for them to acknowledge me.

When they do, I ask, "Everything okay?"

Mom's face is pale, but he stows it away and gives me a false smile. "Marie's not doing well," he informs me.

"Shit, man. I'm sorry to hear that." How long has this been going on? I knew she was in the hospital, but she has been a lot over the years. Hard living will do that to you.

"Me too," he replies, his shoulders slumped in what can only be interpreted as defeat before he collects himself and stands. "I better get back up to the hospital."

"Anything you need, brother. Just call," Judge tells him.

With a nod, Mom slides between us and heads out the door. For a man who's been the backbone of our club, Marie's failing health weighs more heavily on him than anything he's ever had to deal with here.

"How bad is it?" I ask Judge.

"Bad enough. He offered to pass his VP patch to someone who can fulfill the role right now."

Holding an office in our club is sacred. We hold it until we die, or until we're not capable of carrying out our responsibilities. After everything, Judge has never asked for mine back, and Mom's offer to hand it off means Marie isn't going to recover from this.

"Fuck, man. I didn't even know she was that sick. How long has this been going on?"

"Last couple of years. Part of the reason I had him visit the Houston chapter when shit went south was because there were specialists in the area for Marie."

This has been going on for years, and I didn't know? A pang of guilt punches me in the gut. How much else have I missed? How many of my brothers needed support from me and I ignored them?

"Anything I can do to help?"

"Pray for a miracle, because when she goes, I don't know if he'll be able to go on without her. Twenty years together, and fucking cancer is going to tear them apart.

After all the shit we've put them through…" Judge laments with sadness in his voice before turning his focus back on me. "What about you? You good?"

"Yeah," I lie. "Therapy went well."

He eyes me, catching me in the lie, but he lets it go. "Hash has a couple of the garage guys back in his office. Seems they've been getting hit more often."

Over the last few weeks, these guys have been expanding their targets to even more garages around the area, not just the Mom and Pop shops, and we're no closer to figuring out how or why they're doing it. Hash has been pulling all-nighters, analyzing everything he can get his hands on, from camera footage to employee records. They're like ghosts, slipping in and out without so much as a fingerprint or a strand of hair left to identify them.

"How many this time?"

"Six more from the north side of town, and a couple from the suburbs."

I scoff at the number. Dozens of break-ins and zero leads. The local cops have better records than this. If we can't figure it out without means, we're royally screwed.

"We've got to figure this shit out. No one works that clean. What about our eyes and ears around town?"

"Same fucking thing. No one new has rolled into town they've heard about."

"How the fuck does that happen? You don't pull off B&Es like it's a trip to the goddamn grocery store."

"Not a clue. But Hashtag's hoping the new hits will yield something we can work with this time."

"I sure as fuck hope so, for all our sakes. It needs to get back to normal around here."

Silence snakes its way into the conversation, and just as he'd done with Mom, Judge rests his hand on my shoulder.

"That only happens when we all work together, Karma." His words linger between us with an alternative meaning. It leaves me reeling.

Fuck, it's me. All this time, the cause has been staring directly back at me in the mirror. I've been so absorbed in my own fucking problems and self-pity, I didn't see what's been going on around me. I've ignored my club, my brothers. The men I've stood side by side with in battle because I can't get out of my own fucking head. They needed me, and I wasn't there for them in the one way I should've been, my injuries and self-loathing taking complete control of everything in my life.

That's why she's gone, why she left me. I hurt her. More so than I ever thought possible.

My stomach drops when I think about all the pain I've inflicted on her, even before the accident. It wasn't just her graduation party. I've been absent for so long, and she was the only one trying to make it work. To carry the load of our fucked-up relationship. I broke her like I was broken, reshaping and placing her into the same tangled web of pain I've lived in my entire life. A vicious cycle she didn't deserve to be caught up in.

She left because I couldn't give her what she wanted, which was me. The real me. Not the shadow of a man who never truly let her in. The man who should've fought harder to make her stay. Loved her harder, and not thrown the fucking blame everywhere but where it belonged, which was with me.

I'm the problem. That's what Judge meant that night, but my mind wouldn't let me see past all the rage and betrayal. She was right to leave me. She didn't deserve this.

I have to do better, to get better. Not just for her or the club, but for myself. That's the only way out of this.

Pulling my phone from my pocket, I scroll through my contacts and select the number I need. It rings a few times before she picks up.

"Blair, I need help."

Chapter 17

LINDSEY

"SORRY, DARLIN'," Uncle Judge says on the other end of the line. "I know you liked Marie."

"How's Mom?" I ask, shoving the heartbreak of loss down, at least until I get through this conversation.

"Honestly?"

"Honestly."

"Man's a fucking wreck. Even knowing it was coming wasn't enough to cushion that blow. He's gonna need time."

I swallow back the tears. "Are his kids coming home to be with him? I don't like the idea of him being alone."

"He's not alone. He has the club."

I fight the urge to roll my eyes. "You know what I mean. He needs his kids. Last I heard, Tommy was in San Antonio, and Tammy right in Austin, attending beauty school."

"They're already here, honey. Don't you worry about Mom, we have him covered. Probably more than he'd like at this point."

I can only imagine. Mom's called Mom for a reason. Not only does he have a need to make sure everyone else in the club is in a good place, but it takes a lot for him to accept that he too may need help from time to time.

"When's the funeral?"

"In two days. Marie had already set it all up without Mom even knowing. We have no idea how she paid for it all, but you know Marie, always one for the mystery. And she knew Mom would be wrecked. It was the one last thing she could do to take care of him."

I press my lips into a thin, sad smile. "They loved each other."

"They sure did," he agrees. "Weirdest fucking love I've ever seen. But even at their worst, as a team, they were unbreakable."

That just makes me even more sad, proving that no couple is unbreakable. Not really. Even one with a rock-solid foundation like Mom and Marie are susceptible to being destroyed in an instant.

An image of Karma flashes through my mind. It happens a lot throughout the day, every single day, but I've grown accustomed to turning it off. I can't think about him. Not anymore.

"You coming home for it?"

I blink, my mind coming back to the present and to the phone in my hand. "For what?"

"The funeral. Are you going to come home?

"I don't know."

Judge sighs. "No pressure. I get you have... unfinished business here."

That makes me feel like shit. Yeah, I do have unfinished business there, and not just with Karma. I hadn't just left him all those weeks ago. I'd left without a word to Blair as well.

She hadn't done anything to deserve me ghosting her like that besides have the audacity to get pregnant.

God, I'm an asshole.

"I'll talk to my boss. Mom and Marie are more important than anything I may have left unfinished."

He doesn't reply to that, but his question hangs heavy in the air.

"I can't avoid coming home forever. And besides, I miss my family."

I miss everyone.

"Okay, sweetheart. Let me know when you know."

"Will do. Love you, Uncle Judge."

"Love you too, doll face."

Disconnecting the call, I drop my head forward and close my eyes. For just a few moments, I allow my thoughts to drift to Marie, and to all the memories of her and her crazy. She was a pretty awesome chick. You just had to know how to take her.

The world is a little less bright without her in it.

I look around my condo, taking in everything surrounding me. It's nicely decorated, just like my office. But it's nothing like the home I'd grown up in with my uncle, or the one I'd lived in with Karma.

This place is crisp and clean, lacking any personality.

I tried, of course. I'd brought along my books and my framed photos of friends and family. I'd even bought a goldfish the day I'd gone to the mall with Nora.

We'd wandered into the pet store and there he was, all alone in a big tank with no other fish to keep him company. I knew how that felt, and for some reason, I'd decided that fish and I were meant to be friends. So I'd brought him home, along with a small bowl with gravel and a tiny plant.

His name is Harry, and Harry is the first male to ever listen to me without jumping in with his own thoughts or opinions. I don't actually know if Harry is a male or female, but to be honest, I don't care.

Harry is by far the best part of my condo, and he and I get along swimmingly.

I think about going home for the funeral. It's only for two nights. Harry can survive that, I'm sure. It's not Harry I'm worried about, though. It's having to call Mr. Frost and request the time off.

I've spent most of my time at the Institute avoiding Mr. Frost and his advances, which have been many. In fact, he's been pretty forthcoming about his interest in me, even in front of the staff.

I'm not used to that. I grew up like the daughter of a motorcycle club president. Men, or boys, back in the day, knew better than to do anything that might make me uncomfortable. Not only would it not be good with the club, but it was a given that Uncle Judge would see to it they never walked again.

Besides, I don't have an issue with older men, but Abe is pushing sixty years old. Just... ew.

Pulling up his number, I place the call, my stomach sinking like a stone when he answers on the first ring.

"Lindsey, hello." He sounds far too pleased that I'm phoning him after work hours.

I try not to think about that when I explain, "Hello, Mr. Frost. I'm sorry to bother you on your personal time, but I've had something of a family emergency come up."

"Oh, my," he responds, and I can practically hear his bushy eyebrows raising right along with the octave of his voice. "I hope everything is all right."

I worry my lower lip and stare out at the serene water of the lake. "It's not. There's been a death in the family. My aunt. She died of cancer, and I need to go home for the funeral."

Silence reverberates through the phone. "I see," is all

he says when he finally speaks.

"I really just need one day off. Tomorrow's Sunday, so I'm not working, anyway. The funeral is Monday, and I'll be back Tuesday in time for my first appointment at noon."

"Hmmm... Miss Kingston will not be pleased with you cancelling your appointment on Monday."

I blink. How does he know what appointments I have on Monday?

"I'll reschedule her before I leave," I assure him.

"How about you schedule a dinner date with me in there for Tuesday evening, and you've got yourself a deal."

If it was humanly possible for a person's jaw to hit the floor, mine would have. "Sorry?"

"Dinner. With me. Tuesday."

Maybe it's due to the grief I'm feeling, I'm not sure, but that's the last straw.

"Sir, I'll be going home to attend my aunt's funeral. I'll be back in time for my noon appointment on Tuesday, and I will not then, or ever, be going out to dinner with you."

I imagine his eyebrow hairs blowing in the breeze as he lifts them to the ceiling once again, but I don't give him time to respond. Instead, I disconnect the call and set about packing my things to go home and say one final goodbye to crazy, wonderful Marie.

Chapter 18

KARMA

MARIE'S DEATH has cast a dark cloud over the club. An inky smudge of grief staining us all.

In the couple of days since she died, I'd learned so much about her and her life with Mom. Their kids. Her life in the club. How she used to be the life of all the club parties, and was crazier than anyone else here, man or woman. That she had the biggest heart. And more importantly, she was Mom's backbone, and now she's fucking gone. A void that many will be unable to fill for the rest of their lives.

Meeting with Blair over the last week has been eye opening for me, giving me a perspective into what I'd missed over the last few years, even though it was playing out right in front of me. It was like I had chosen to ignore it all.

Before, I wouldn't have given two shits about a

funeral for someone I really didn't know outside of her husband being in my club, stuffing myself into a dress shirt and slacks for his benefit, and not out of mourning. Today, I stand here with my brothers in support of not only Mom and his family, but for all of us. *My* family.

Their kids flanking him on either side, Mom's frame is stoic as he approaches her casket, but his shoulders slump visibly the closer he gets, his daughter sobbing against his arm. A steady stream of people come into the room over the course of visiting hours. Friends, family, members of our club from other chapters, all fill the room, but there's one person I wish were here, and that's Lindsey.

She loved Marie. They'd always had a bond I couldn't explain, and I wish I had taken the time to understand it now. She'd hate herself for missing this chance to say her last goodbye.

Judge told me he had called her, but she didn't indicate whether she would be attending the services or not. I'd offered to stay behind if that meant she would come, but Judge had dismissed the idea immediately. We're all Mom's family, and we all needed to be here. And if she did show up, his orders were clear. Stay the hell away from her.

"You all right, K?" GP asks when he joins me at the far end of the room.

"Yeah, man. Just thinking about some shit. Where's Blair? I thought she'd be here."

He arches his brow in slight surprise at my mentioning his old lady.

"She's back at the clubhouse, making sure the meal is ready with Grace and Shelby." Marie's job. Her mantle being taken up by our newest old ladies. "They came by earlier to give their respects."

The funeral director, clad in his black suit and tie, draws my attention when he moves to the front of the room and clears his throat.

"For those of you who wish to stay for the memorial service, we will begin in the next fifteen minutes. We ask at that time, each of you stay seated until the conclusion of the service. There will be no graveside services, but a dinner will be held if you'd like to join Marie's family afterward. Thank you."

He walks off to the side and begins talking to the older woman who'd been helping him when we got here.

"Better find a seat."

I start to follow him, when someone walking in from the back grabs my attention. There, in a tight black dress and heels that show off every curve of her body, is Lindsey.

She's here.

She searches the room until she sees Mom and her

uncle standing up near the front and moves toward them, her eyes focused solely on them. I can only watch as she passes directly in front of me, only a yard between us.

Horror brews inside of me. *What's happened to my woman?*

She's lost weight since she left. Too much if you ask me. Her curves were the kind that guys dreamed about. The roundness of her cheeks is slightly sunken in, and dark rings circle her eyes. Her normally long, brunette hair is cut to her chin, and hangs in curls along her face. I fucking hate it. She always loved her hair long, and so did I. But a lot has changed in the last month, it seems, for the both of us.

Judge notices her and heads in her direction. I stand frozen as she wraps her thin arms around his neck and hugs him tightly. Looking over her shoulder, he narrows his eyes at me and I nod, remembering his warning. Judge then tucks her under his shoulder in a protective way and leads her up to Mom, her body trembling by the time she reaches the casket. Without looking over, Mom knows she's there, and he pulls her close.

I stay where I am, giving her space, despite my brain pushing me to go up there and take her in my arms. Watching her cry against Mom's shoulder is fucking killing me. I want to comfort her in her grief, but she's not here for me. She's here for Mom. I won't ruin that for them in my selfishness to be near her. All I can do is watch from a distance and hope she's okay.

The funeral director comes back to the front of the room, and she settles into a seat next to Judge. I move up so I'm just a few rows behind her.

A Baptist minister comes to the front of the room, but everything he says falls on deaf ears. The only person I can focus on is her. I watch her every move, looking for any sign that she misses me, but she never looks back.

I should be up there with her.

The service is short, and before I know it, the funeral director dismisses each row to give our final respects. I can feel Lindsey's gaze on me when I walk by and sneak a glance. She's worse off than I thought. No amount of make-up can hide the hollow sadness in her eyes. She's suffering, and it only intensifies my need to reach out to her.

She's not ready yet. Give her space. Give her time.

Blair's words from our last talk yesterday ring in my head. She's right, I know that, but I'd really rather she be fucking wrong.

I move past them, giving Mom and his kids my condolences again before exiting the viewing room and heading outside. A group of my brothers gather around their bikes, but I go straight for my truck and watch the family as they leave last, Lindsey with them. Everyone gets in their cars, and Judge leads Lindsey to his bike.

Once they're ready to go, Judge rides out with the rest of the club behind him, and me bringing up the rear.

She should be riding with me.

Anger stirs just under the surface the longer I drive. I'd been doing so well the last few weeks, and seeing her once is starting to make me lose the razor thin control I had built up between my talks with Blair and physical therapy. I have to rein it in.

A line of traffic bottlenecks at the entrance to the clubhouse. When I finally manage to get in and park, most of the crowd is already inside. I consider staying out here, or even just leaving and going the hell home, but Judge would have my ass. It doesn't matter, because I need to be close to her, even if it is from a distance.

Trudging away from my truck, I head inside. The couches have been moved, and the area is now filled with rows of tables. The mouthwatering aroma of expertly cooked brisket wafts in through the open back door.

I peer around, looking for Lindsey, but she's nowhere in sight. I start for the hallway when Hashtag calls out from the bar.

"Want a brew?"

"Nah, man, I'm good. Still on pain meds."

He gives me an incredulous look. "You get body snatched or something? Never seen you turn down a brew."

"Trying to behave."

He lets out a gut-busting laugh. "You almost had me there a second, K." Sliding the beer toward me, he bends down to grab another one for himself. I leave mine sitting there, opting to keep my promise, and start for my room in the hallway nearby, but stop dead in my tracks. Standing just outside the kitchen door is Lindsey.

"Fuck it," I growl under my breath, not bothering to consider the consequences. I just go.

She doesn't see me coming at her until it's too late. She lets out a startled yelp when I grab her by the elbow and march her straight into the closest room I can find. It's the fucking utility closet, but it's quiet, and nobody else is in here, which makes it kind of perfect. Reaching up, I click on the light.

"What the fuck do you think you're doing?" she snarls. "Let me out of here."

I step back, but stay the course I hadn't intended to take tonight.

"Not until I tell you what I have to say."

She rolls her eyes. "We've said everything we need to say to each other."

"Bullshit, Lins. Bull-fucking-shit. You left without a word. Nothing was said at all."

She starts to take in the room, likely searching for a way to escape. But she can't hide from me here. It's just us. The way I've wanted it to be for weeks now.

"It's over between us, Karma, and it's high time you accept it and move on." She goes to step around me, her hand going for the handle, and something in me snaps.

In one swift move, I take her hand and spin her around, pinning it against the wall high above her head.

Lindsey's breath comes out in puffs that billow over my lips, her chest heaving, but she doesn't say a word. Her eyes are glued to mine.

"Hands up," I growl, taking a step back.

She doesn't argue. Doing exactly what she's told, she raises her other hand and presses it to the wall above her head, her eyes shifting from angry to burning.

"Spread your legs."

Pressing her shoulder blades into the wall, she keeps her hands put and spreads her feet apart on the floor, her heels making little clicks that make my cock twitch.

"You wearing panties, baby?"

She nods.

"Answer me."

Swallowing, she replies, "Yes."

I shake my head in disappointment and lean forward, trailing the tips of my fingers along the inside of her thigh, raising her little black dress as I go.

"You know I don't like it when you have panties on, don't you?"

Her response is breathy, barely audible. "Yes."

Her skin is like silk beneath my touch, and my cock is straining to be set free. To have her.

"Were you trying to make me angry, Lindsey?"

"No."

God, I've fucking missed this. This is our thing. Our kink.

She's been submissive to me since before we even tried to be together. She can be a ballbuster, but whenever there's sex involved, she's putty in my hands.

Dropping to my knees, I bury my face between her legs and breathe her in. Fucking Christ. She smells better than I remember.

Her panties are damp.

Slowly, I move my nose from side to side, feeling her sweet, sensitive clit roll beneath it, and listen as she whimpers.

"You want me to kiss you here, baby?"

"Yes."

I nip her clit gently through the lacy fabric. "You want me to suck this sweet pussy?"

"God, yes," she hisses.

"Pull your panties aside, Lindsey. Offer it to me."

My heart thrums in my chest as she lowers her hand and hooks a single finger under the thin fabric between her legs and pulls it aside.

I want to play it cool, to make her squirm. I want to make her scream my name a million times before she finally tumbles over the edge. But I've fucking missed Lindsey so goddamn much, and her perfect pussy is pouting right in front of me.

So I do the only thing I can do.

I bury my face in it. With the flat of my tongue, I lap at her clit, reveling in how fast her breathing gets. With one hand, I lift her leg up over my shoulder, angling her hips to give me better access.

I fucking drown myself in her sex, sucking and licking and kissing. I fuck her pussy with my mouth, drawing out every ounce of pleasure I can.

My balls are like rocks inside of my pants, and I know I'm not going to last. It's been a long fucking time since we've had each other. And not only that, this is Lindsey.

I can't take it another second.

Pulling back, I pop onto my feet and wrestle with the buckle on my belt. "Pull those tits out, gorgeous. I miss them too."

She grins, a sexy flush moving from her chest to her cheeks as she pulls down the front of her dress, displaying her beautiful breasts for me.

Grabbing her hips, I lift her, placing her right on my cock.

Her pussy fits over me like a glove, encasing every inch of me. Our groans mingle as I fill her.

And then I move.

My eyes never leave hers as I lift her breast with one

hand and lave it with my tongue, my hips thrusting me in and out between her legs.

Her moans turn to cries, and I know I'm about to blow.

I try to think of anything to last just a little longer, but her pussy's like silk, and the look in her eyes as I use my mouth on her tit does me in.

With a gentle, but firm bite to her nipple, I slam into her one last time. Her fingernails dig into my shoulders as she trembles through her release, but I barely notice.

My own release washes over me like a tidal wave. And as we wade through it together, I slide my tongue into her mouth, creating a perfect tornado of flesh and desire.

We kiss like that long after our climax. I don't even want to put her down. I want to stay buried inside of her forever, a slave to her pussy and her heart.

When she pulls away, I place her gently onto her feet and take a step back.

"This doesn't change a thing. You know that, right?" she whispers, shoving her dress down over her hips. "It was a one-time thing."

Fuck that. "That's where you're wrong, baby. You and me are never a one-time thing. End game, remember?"

"Maybe before everything happened, sure, but we're different people now."

"Things change, Lindsey. People change. You may

not believe it, but this isn't over. I'm working through my shit so I can be the man you need me to be."

The sad look in her eyes breaks my heart. "It's too late for all that, Karma."

"It's not," I argue, keeping my voice calm. "One day, you'll see I'm worthy of you, and I promise, that day will come. But baby, you have to let me back in so I can prove it to you."

Her face softens for a split second before she puts up her walls again. "I wish I could believe you."

"You can," I insist. "Can I call you?"

She adjusts her dress one last time and turns toward the door.

"Yes."

She steps out into the hallway, leaving me there in the dim light.

My heart soars, and a glimmer of hope takes root. Maybe I can fix this shit between us once and for all.

Chapter 19

LINDSEY

I STARE DOWN at the phone on my coffee table, lit up like a Christmas tree.

Karma.

I know I told him he could call, but I hadn't completely come to grips with the fact that when he did, I'd have to talk to him.

It sounds stupid, I know, but I've spent so long burying my feelings for him down deep, stomping on them whenever they rose too close to the surface just so I could make it through the day.

Some psychologist I am.

With my finger trembling, I reach out and tap the screen to accept the call.

"Hello?"

There's a brief pause, as if he's just as surprised as I am that I'd actually answered.

"Lindsey, hey. How are you?"

"Uh…" God, why is this so hard? "Hey. Yeah, um… I'm good."

He lets out a low chuckle that causes a tiny flutter in my belly. "Fuckin' hell. I didn't think it would be so weird."

I mull that over. I didn't think it would be this weird, either. So what does it mean that it is? Are we pushing it? Are we trying too hard?

Maybe I just need to go with the original plan of zero contact after all.

"Twat Knot got caught banging some old broad in the bathroom at Sharkey's."

I cough out an unexpected laugh. "What?"

"Yeah. Fucking guy." Karma's laugh is easy, and it's surprising just how much it relaxes me. "Bunch of us went out to Sharkey's last night. Needed a change of scenery, ya know?"

I do know. Marie was a permanent fixture at the Black Hoods' clubhouse. Her presence was always noticeable and would be sorely missed.

"Anyway, there's this group of women there. You know the type. Cougars, really. Make-up overdone, hair hard as a rock because they've put so much junk in it. And shirts that show off their fake tans and wrinkled chests."

I giggle, because without intending to, he'd just

described Marie herself.

"So they're out there, dancing and drinking, and hooting at all the young boys. One of 'em even pinched Priest's ass."

My giggle turns into a full-on laugh.

"Halfway through the night, TK disappears. We figured he'd just gone home with some chick like he always does."

It's true. Twat Knot is a total slut. He'd fuck anyone who would let him, as long as they had a nice set of boobs.

"I've downed about a million sodas, so I head for the bathroom. I open the door, and there they are. He had the old bitty up on the dirty ass counter, just slamming it into her. Her tits were sagging down into her armpits and flopping all over the place, but he didn't even slow down."

This breaks me. I laugh so hard, my sides ache. I know I need to go back and revisit that whole drinking soda thing, but right now, all I can picture is Twat Knot nailing somebody's poor old grandma.

"Oh, God," I cry, wiping away a tear. "Lucky you to be the one to have that vision burned into your memory."

Karma scoffs. "I'll never be able to look at an old lady again without imagining that terrifying little scene."

I can't contain the giggles that overtake me. "What did Twat Knot say?" I manage to ask.

"Stupid fucker thought it was awesome. Said the old bird had a Mercedes, and that she knew how to suck a dick. Told me older women come with more experience."

This makes me howl. I can't remember the last time I laughed this hard. It's been ages.

Leave it to Twat Knot to provide the pervy comedic story to break that.

Flopping back on my couch, the laughter slowly fades along with Karma's.

"I miss you, Lindsey," he says after a long, comfortable silence.

"I miss you too," I whisper.

Someone calls his name in the background, and I know he's gonna have to go.

"Call you tomorrow? Same time?"

"Okay."

"Unless you have plans," he drawls out, attempting to sound like he's teasing. But it's clear he's fishing for information, something I'm not quite ready to share with him.

Harry's fishbowl catches my eye.

I tell him in a casual tone, trying not to giggle, "I'll be around. My only plans are to sit around and watch a movie with Harry."

"Who is Harry?"

"A friend," I answer airily, singing out the words. I know damn well he's thinking Harry is a man, and one I spend my Wednesday evenings watching movies with. I'm not gonna lie when I say I find it extremely hilarious. "Anyway, it was really great talking to you. You go do what you have to do, and we can chat a little more tomorrow."

He wants to argue. I can hear it in the way he says, "Yeah." There's a pause, and I hear Judge calling Karma's name this time. "Till tomorrow."

I can picture him now, sitting in the clubhouse, trying to keep this call private, but having the guys all around him. It makes me miss home.

"Bye, Karma."

"Bye, baby."

When the call disconnects, I stare down at the phone. I never would've guessed how soothing a call from Karma would be, but it's also stirred up a lot of dust that had settled shortly after I left Austin in the first place.

I miss that man. I miss my home. I miss the club and the city.

But my life is here now, so what's the point? Karma will never leave Austin. He loves it there, and he loves his club. He'd never even consider moving chapters.

So if we were to reconnect and get back together, either I'd have to give up this job, or we'd have to remain long distance. Could we even do that?

God, it would be so hard to be with him, but be miles and miles apart. To be jealous of every single person he comes into contact with, just because they get to be near him and I don't.

Besides, Karma'd had a lot of things to work through when I left. Had he done all that? Was he still going to physio?

It makes me sad to think I don't even know the answers to those questions. I used to be an expert in all things Karma. He'd been right when he said we were end game.

But was that game over now? Could we still salvage what we'd had?

I guess time would tell.

KARMA

"YOU'VE GOT to be fucking kidding me," Judge roar when he throws open the overhead door for one of the bays. Hashtag and I give each other a look before heading inside.

The place is a fucking wreck. Parts boxes and tools litter the ground around his feet. *Fuck. We've been hit again.* He kicks at a few of the boxes around his feet, sending them flying in all directions.

"I thought V was here last night."

"Do you see him?" Judge seethes. "He had one fucking job, and he couldn't do that right. I want his cut. Today. I don't give a shit what his excuse is. He's done."

Judge kicks through several more boxes and stomps off toward the back room, accompanied by more swearing.

"I hate to be V when Judge finds his ass." Smirking, Hashtag glides his index finger across his throat.

"Ain't gonna be pretty."

Reaching for my phone, I fire off a text in the group chat, letting the club know they've been back. A few replies trickle in immediately, telling me they're on their way.

"I'll check the cameras and start getting this place cleaned up before Judge throws out a hip kicking these boxes around."

Hashtag grabs his phone and starts thumbing through the feeds.

Stalking around the room, I look for anything to either identify these fuckers, or what could've happened to V. The hair on the back of my neck prickles the longer I look around. Something's off, but I can't put my finger on it. V is relatively new to our chapter. A tagalong product of Mom's trip to Houston to straighten out one of our sister chapters that'd had a major drug problem a few months back. V fit right in for all I knew.

Backtracking, I start at the front of the building. The entrance, just like Hash had described before, shows no signs of forced entry. No scruffs. No tool marks. No broken glass. It's like they just turned the handle and walked right in, or were let in.

V's not capable of this kind of betrayal, is he?

I pull up Priest's number. They're buddies, and last I

heard, they were sharing an apartment near the club-house. It takes a few rings, but he finally answers.

"Someone better be dead for calling at this hour," he growls before checking the caller ID. "Shit, K, my bad. How's my favorite asshole this morning?"

"Where's your buddy at, Priest?"

"V? He's not here. He's at the shop."

"We're at the garage, and the fucker's nowhere to be found."

"I saw him there with my own eyes just a couple of hours ago. Dropped him off a pizza and some energy drinks to keep his ass awake. Are you sure he's not just out back or something?"

"If he's here, he's a fucking ghost. What time was that?"

"Around midnight. I left about three. He was sitting at the office desk watching Golden Girls on his phone when last I saw him."

He was watching what? Yeah, I'm going to forget I heard that.

Turning, I head for the office. On the desk sit a couple of empty energy drink cans and a pizza box. Priest's account is checking out so far, except for the fact he's not fucking here.

"You sure about that time?"

"Yeah, man. I was pissed because I wanted to hit up

that Chinese spot I like on the way home, and they were closed. Is something up?"

"The place has been flipped. Again."

"That can't be right. Are you sure?"

Judge roars again from the back room, and a loud crash echoes through the open building.

"That enough proof for you? If he calls you, I'm the first person you tell. Got it, prospect?"

"Yeah, man. Anything you say."

"Keep me posted."

Hashtag looks up from his phone, just as Judge comes out of the back, his chest heaving. Sliding my phone back into my pocket, I approach him cautiously. Judge has a short fuse, and I'm not about to set that thing off again. He's already riled up enough as it is.

"Please tell me one of you found something."

"Cameras went fuzzy around four thirty this morning. Came back online about fifteen minutes later. The fuckers jammed the signal."

"Don't those things send out alerts for shit like that?" I ask.

"They're supposed to, but there's an alarm delay built into them to detect issues."

"Let me guess," Judge remarks, pinching the bridge of his nose. "It's fifteen minutes or more."

Hashtag nods. "I don't understand how they figured

that shit out. These aren't general public cameras. They're government grade."

"Well, they did." Judge looks over at me. "I guess you got nothin'."

"Called Priest. He was here last night with V and left around three. Swears he was here."

"So we have cameras that didn't do shit, and a prospect who either fucked off his job or is missing."

"Seems to be the case. Sounds like Priest is right, though. V's not here, and neither is his bike."

"That's fucking great. We got nothing, just like the last time. I'm really starting to get tired of this shit."

"Feeling's mutual, Prez. What do you want me to do?"

"Find V."

Nodding, I turn and head for my truck when I hear the crunching of the gravel drive. The shop doesn't open for a couple more hours, so why would someone be driving down the lane at this time of the morning? The engine isn't loud enough to be anyone we're expecting. They'd be riding a motorcycle.

Stepping back, closer to the building's edge, I push against the side wall and wait. Three black vans pull up single file outside the shop, their brakes squealing as they come to a stop right out front.

"We got company, Prez," I yell through the open door.

Reaching for my gun, I hug the wall, pushing myself out of sight. All three sliding doors on the vans pop open, and a dozen men clad in green and black pour out into the parking lot. Most of them are teenagers, and armed to the fucking teeth.

The fucking Ladrones. A street gang we'd run out of Texas years ago after breaking up their drug supply lines. At least I thought we did. How in the hell did we not know they were back in town?

An older man with tattoos all up his throat walks to the front of the mob, smirking at Judge and Hashtag, whose guns are leveled in his direction. His dark black hair is covered in a green and black bandana, and a slew of gold chains hanging from around his neck. I don't recognize him from the last run-in. Not that we had left many of them breathing.

Casually catching my eye, Judge signals with a slight nod for me to stay where I am.

"Shop's not open," Judge says, his voice calm and cool, considering the number of firearms pointing directly at him.

"We're not here for repairs, *homes*," the man drawls, raising his hand up in the air and giving a three-finger wave.

A few of the guys behind him part like the sea, show-casing the sliding door of one of their vans. Inside, an assault rifle pressed against his temple, is V, beaten all to hell. His arms are tied behind his back, blood coating his bruised face. He looks at Judge through one swollen eye, but doesn't try to say anything around the filthy rag tied over his mouth.

Walking over to V, the leader grabs him by the hair and jerks his head back. "I think this belongs to you. Followed us home last night."

The man behind him shoves V out of the van and onto the ground with a boot to his spine. V cries out when he lands, the assault rifle still aimed at him.

"I'll fucking kill you," Hashtag seethes, rushing forward. Judge throws his massive arm out, stopping him in his tracks. We're outnumbered and outgunned. He's playing it smart. They haven't noticed me yet, and the rest of the club should be here soon. He's stalling until they can get here.

"Thank you for bringing him back. Now get the fuck out of here."

"Can't do that," the man tsks, resting his heavy boot on V's back. "One of my members is missing. Word on the street is, you might know something about that."

"Oh yeah? And what is the word, exactly?"

"That a couple of your men took one of mine. Haven't heard from him in a while." The leader smirks. "I tried asking your little friend here, but he seems to be having trouble getting the words out. We may have had a bit of fun with him."

Rage consumes me as he grinds his foot between V's shoulder blades, but I hold my position.

My teeth grind together the longer I watch from the shadows, waiting for a sign from Judge to move in. The odds aren't in our favor, even with me coming in as a surprise. But at least I could add more firepower to our side of the playing field.

The cold metal of a gun barrel presses to the back of my skull, making my blood run cold.

"Give me your gun," a male voice growls into my ear. Snatching it out of my hands, he shoves me forward. "Join your friends."

He follows close behind me until I'm next to Judge, front and center of their firing squad.

"Welcome," the man standing on V's back quips when we stop. "Look at this big motherfucker. Bet you're just itching to get your buddy here back."

A few of his guys chuckle behind him, and I have to suck in a deep breath, trying to shove down the fury raging inside of me. Before the shooting, I may have been able to take out quite a few of these fuckers. But now, I'd be lucky if I could get through more than a couple of them. We need the rest of the club here. It's the only way we walk out of here alive.

"Enough!" Judge barks, taking a step forward, moving the attention off of me and back on him. "What the fuck do you assholes want?"

"I like you, old man. Straight to the fucking point." He taps his gun against his chest. "My predecessor was right about you. Too bad we aren't on the same side. We could work well together."

Judge's expression never changes. "Not fucking likely. Get to the point."

The man lifts his foot from V's back and steps away from him. "I have a deal that might interest you."

A deal? A deal was a conversation between a couple of people from each side. Not a dozen well-armed men and a hostage. There isn't a deal to be had here.

"What kind of deal?"

He nods down at V. "Him."

Judge holds steady. "In exchange for what?"

"For you to stay the fuck out of our business."

Judge lets out a mirthless chuckle. "How does that benefit me? Say I take it. You'll just keep robbing us fucking blind, and then we're back to this shit all over again."

"That's the sweetener, my friend," the man replies, his smile growing wider. "You and the rest of your leather wearing assholes stay away from us, and I'll make sure your shop is off-limits."

I stifle a laugh. *Bullshit.*

Judge appears to consider this. "What's the guarantee you won't go back on this so-called deal of yours?"

The man just shrugs. "I guess there's not one. But

there's no other option for you, my friend." He begins to pace in front of us. "Say yes, we leave, and our business is done. Say no, and well, I think you know what will happen." The cocking of every single firearm echoes behind him.

Judge glances between Hashtag and me. There's a fire in his eyes that tells me all I need to know, but there's something more behind it. Something I like.

"Fine," Judge replies after a couple of minutes.

The man laughs. "I knew you'd see it my way."

The rumble of motorcycles reverberates from down the lane. The cavalry is almost fucking here.

"I think it's time for us to go, gentlemen." His men start filing back into the vans, but he stays outside next to V until the last man is loaded inside.

"Remember our deal, old man." Popping open the passenger side door of the closest van, he slips inside and bangs his hand on the side. They head out as one, kicking up dust like a fucking tornado.

As soon as they're out of sight, I rush toward V and fall to my knees beside him. The gravel digs into my skin, but I don't fucking care. Turning him onto his back, he lets out a ragged breath, just as the rest of our crew arrive. Priest is off his bike without really stopping and joins me next to V.

"Who did this do him?"

"The fuck's going on here?" GP growls.

"We had visitors," Judge replies. "The motherfucking Ladrones."

GP's eyes go wide. "When the fuck did they get back into town?"

"Good question. But they're here, and they're the ones hitting all the garages." Judge gives the guys the rundown of the conversation we had with them and the army they brought.

The bottom line doesn't look good. We're outnumbered at least three to one. If they have this much manpower for a power play, they've got more elsewhere.

"Fuck!" GP hisses, running his hand in frustration through his hair. "What's the plan, Prez?"

Judge turns away from looking over V to address the rest of us. "Fuck their deal. We kill every last one of these fuckers, starting with their leader. This ends, now."

LINDSEY

"PICK UP, PICK UP, PICK UP," I mutter into my phone as it rings relentlessly.

I don't know what's going on, but I've had the worst feeling all afternoon. I'd tried to call Uncle Judge a few times, but the calls went straight to voicemail. Grace had been no help. She was used to him going dark when shit was happening with the club.

Truth be told, so am I. But this just feels different somehow.

Karma's automated voicemail speaks to me from the other end. Again. This time, I leave a message.

"Hey, it's Lindsey. I, uh, just wanted to see how you're doing. Give me a call when you get a sec."

I disconnect the call, feeling like a total ass. Why did I even call? Karma and I had spoken a couple of times in the last few days, but he'd always been the one to make contact.

What does me calling say to him? That I'm ready to get back together? That I'm upset he hasn't called yet?

I roll my eyes. *Jesus, Lins, calm down. Stop overthinking it.*

But Karma hadn't answered, either, and that sinking feeling still weighs heavy in my gut.

I look down at my phone, knowing exactly who I should call next. Blair.

But since the night of my graduation, I hadn't spoken with her at all. I'd practically forced her to announce her pregnancy. I'd freaked, and up and moved cities completely without a word.

In the beginning, she called at least once a day, and texted too. Then gradually, the calls had stopped, and the texts had changed from every day to every few days, to once a week. And now, I hadn't heard from her in almost ten days.

I'd read every text, yet never answered a single one.

Pride is a funny thing. Having pride in yourself can be a wonderful thing. It's almost a virtue to be able to hold your head high and be proud of your own hard work and successes.

But it can also consume you, holding you tight in its destructive clutches. Pride can steal your joy and destroy your relationships. And that's exactly what had happened with Blair.

I'd acted so selfish that night, and now that so much time has passed, I know I have to eat a pretty healthy serving of humble pie to make up for it. Blair did nothing wrong. The issue was never her.

It had been my relationship with Karma that had sent me running, and the absolutely awful way in which I'd handled it.

Swallowing down the giant lump in my throat, I pull up Blair's number and hit the button before I can talk myself out of it.

"Oh my God!" she squeals, answering before the second ring. "Lindsey, hi!"

My eyes burn with tears as soon as she says my name, and I hiccup out an unexpected sob.

"Oh, Blair. I'm so sorry."

"Honey, no." Her voice changes from excited to compassionate. "No sorries needed, okay? I get it, I do. I'm just glad you're calling me now."

I continue to sob, nodding my head as if she can see me.

"You still with me?"

Drawing in a shaky breath, I manage to say, "Yes."

After a minute more of listening to me cry, she says, "Look, let me make this easy on you. You're sorry for ditching me at the party and not talking to me since. You had a lot going on between you and Karma, and you never really meant to take it out on me. You found out I was expecting, and all that did was remind you of the baby you'd lost. Now it's been forever, and you just haven't known how to make contact. Did I miss anything?"

I snag a tissue from the box beside my couch and wipe the tears as they fall off the tip of my nose and chuckle. God, I've missed her.

"That about covers it."

"Good. Now, next topic. How's Houston?"

I snuggle into the couch. "Okay, for the most part. My condo is awesome, and my office is extra posh. But my boss is a pervert, my clients need their trust funds taken away, and there's no you."

"Sounds awful," she deadpans, and then we both bust out in laughter.

For just a second, I forget about that awful feeling I've been having today, and I forget about how long it's been since I'd spoken with her. It's just Blair and me, and I've missed her so damn much.

Once the laughter dies down, the smile slowly fades from my lips. "I am sorry, you know."

"I know."

"I am happy for you and GP. When are you due?"

"Four months from today, actually."

I smile. Not long at all. "Do we know what we're having yet?"

"Nope." She pops the last syllable in a way that tells me GP had wanted to know, but Blair wanted it to be a surprise. Blair won, obviously.

"You know, you will have kids too someday."

Her words are like a punch in the gut, stealing my air away in an instant. It takes me a moment before I finally tell her, "No. I can't. You know that."

"Honey, there's more than one way to complete your family. You'll have yours. It may not be the way you'd always thought it would be, but you will have your family someday."

I feel the tears beginning to form again, but I beat them back. "I hope so."

We both go silent, and it's Blair who breaks it. "He's working hard, you know."

"Who?"

"Karma. He's really putting in an honest effort to get better. He's determined to get you back."

This surprises me. Karma isn't an overly chatty guy, and he doesn't exactly spend a lot of time having heart to hearts with his brothers old ladies.

"He spoke to you about it?"

"He didn't tell you?"

My frown deepens. "Tell me what?"

"Karma comes to see me a couple times a week. He won't go to a therapist, but says he's comfortable keeping it in the family. I can't tell you what we talk about, obviously, but I can tell you that man loves you very much. And he knows exactly what needs to be done to make things right."

My heart skips a beat. I can't believe he's been talking to Blair, like as an actual therapist.

I desperately want to know more, but I know damn well she can't tell me anything. Instead, I focus on why I'd called in the first place.

"I can't get ahold of my uncle or Karma. Do you know if everything's okay?"

"All I know is, they're still dealing with whatever's going on with the break-ins at the local garages. Even theirs has been hit. They're likely doing something we're better off not knowing about."

"Yeah, true." When it comes to the MC, the old saying is true. Ignorance actually is bliss.

"So, when are you coming home?"

And that's how I spend the next hour of my day, catching up with Blair, finding out all the gossip from school and the town. Discussing nursery colors and baby names. Talking about ideas for the shelter she'd started earlier in the year.

By the time we get off the phone, my heart is full, and I'm missing home more than ever.

KARMA

AFTER GETTING V to the hospital, we realized just how lucky he was to survive. Broken jaw, multiple broken ribs, and a brain bleed. The Ladrones had done a number on him. And seeing just how close we were to losing him only stoked the fire for revenge. With Priest babysitting him at the hospital, we were down even more in numbers, especially since Mom is on a bit of a bereavement, trying to tie up Marie's affairs and process losing her in the first place. And Stone Face has been flaky as fuck lately.

"Any new updates on V?" Burnt asks as we all sit down at our table. The room's so empty, our voices almost echo.

"He's stable, according to Priest. Doctor's hadn't yet been in today," TK offers.

"What did y'all tell the doctors?" Burnt drawls.

"Accident."

I cringe at the thought of calling his beating an accident. He was doing the job Judge gave him, and he'd more than paid the price for it. A pang of guilt hits hard, thinking I had considered he was slacking off on his job for even a second.

"Think they bought it?"

"We paid them enough not to give a fuck either way."

Did they do this when I was in the hospital? Constant updates? A prospect guarding me? Those first few days were only a blur, but the one constant I knew was next to me was Lindsey. Part of me wishes she were here right now, but she'd be in danger. I have to focus on these fuckers first.

"Stable is good news," Judge adds, shuffling toward his seat at the head of the table. His gray hair and beard seem lighter than before these fuckers started messing with the garages.

"Let's get started. We've got a lot to cover this morning."

The guys settle in around the table. I take in the group, noting how our numbers are dwindling. As the original chapter, we should be the biggest, but here we are, a skeleton crew.

"You all know what we need to do. The Ladrones coming back into our territory is a major problem. The first time they were here, they flooded the streets with shit drugs, and now they're going after local businesses. We only have one option."

"Eradicate these fuckers," Hashtag snorts. "But it's not going to be easy." Taking a file from his lap, he slides it across the table.

"What's all this?"

"About four cups of the world's strongest coffee and calling in some favors. Word on the street is, they rolled in about the time we were dealing with the dog ring. Came in quiet. Started boosting their numbers with local runaways."

"How many do you think they have?"

"I can't be sure, but my source is saying dozens."

Shit. "Seven against dozens? We're going to need one hell of a plan."

"No shit," TK throws into the discussion. "No offense, K, but there's really just six of us."

Judge drags his thumb over his chin. "I think we need to consider calling in a couple more chapters. More boots on the ground."

"Which chapters?" Twat Knot asks. "Houston's still recovering from their little drug problem. Dallas has the numbers, but they're inexperienced."

"San Marcos," I propose. "They've got the numbers and a vested interest. We let them clean house here, they'll just move farther south."

"Make the calls. Put Houston and San Antonio on

alert. We may need them to be on call to circle the family wagons if shit goes south."

GP clears his throat. "I agree with that, but how do we keep it under the radar? They'll notice more of us in town."

"It's a risk. They could come without their colors and in some cages. That might throw off the scent," Hashtag considers. "But there's a bigger problem than that. We have no idea where these guys are holed up. I've got some of our sources around town snooping, but it's not like the last time. These fuckers are underground."

"Our only option is to flush them out. Dangle a cookie they'll want a bite of." A few of the guys start grumbling. "It's all we have. Smoke them out of their hole and take them when they least expect it."

"How do you want to do this, Prez?"

"Put the word out on the street that there's a shipment of high-end parts coming into a shop in town. Have a couple of the San Marcos guys drive it up, and we'll Trojan horse the shit out of it. Have a group of us in the truck, and the rest in the surrounding area."

"You sure that's going to work?" Burnt leans forward on his elbows. "They've been ahead of us every step of the damn way."

"We've tried new shit, and it hasn't done a thing to stop them. It's time to bring out some old tricks for new pups. You got any other ideas?"

Burnt leans back in his seat, crossing his arms over his chest. "I might, but it's going to take time."

"We don't have time," I growl. "Look at what they did to V. Do you think they'll fucking hesitate to do that to you? What about the kids? The women? We have to draw the line in the sand somewhere, and I'm fucking drawing it now."

Judge looks over at me with pride slipping through the hardened cracks on his face.

"Karma's right. We do this now. Put the calls in and get them here ASAP."

A crash from the main room grabs my attention, as well as the others. Burnt and TK shift from their seats and stalk quietly toward the door where someone's humming from the other side.

"Honey, I'm home." A slurred voice sings out. Judge goes rigid as Stone Face walks in and leans against the doorframe, smiling like a sadistic fucking clown. "Can I join your tea party, ladies?"

He looks like shit. Maybe more like shit warmed over and hit by a semi and backed over. This fucker has been living hard.

"You're late," Judge grunts.

"And you're an asshole," he fires right back. Stone Face takes a few steps and stumbles, catching himself on the table.

Judge heads toward him, being sure not to move too fast.

"How much have you had to drink, son?"

He beams up at Judge. "Not enough."

"By the smell and look of you, it appears you stumbled into a barrel of whiskey."

"Maybe I did. What's it to you?" You'd think he was eight years old. A very large, very hairy, and very drunk eight-year-old. "You're not the boss of me."

"You're a part of this club, asshole. I became your boss when I patched you in. You know the rules."

"Fuck your rules, and fuck you."

At the murderous expression on Judge's face, I push back from my chair and get in between them. Normally this shit wouldn't phase Judge in the slightest. He'd wait to lose his shit until Stone Face was sober enough to hear it.

"Easy, big guy," I croon, slipping Stone Face's massive arm up and over my shoulder. "Let's go get you some coffee. You're not thinking straight."

Judge steps back, giving me space to help his bumbling ass out the door and into the main room. The big fucker takes the opportunity and leans on me with all his weight, and I hear an audible *pop* as my knee nearly gives way.

"Get him the fuck out of here and sober his ass up," Judge snaps.

"Will do, Prez."

It takes a few tries, but we make it out the door.

"You're an asshole," Stone Face states.

"Tell me something I didn't already know." In response, he leans more of his weight on me. "How about you try walking on your own two feet?"

He rolls his head over and onto my shoulder. "How about you go get me another beer?"

I maneuver him down the hallway, away from the bar.

"Hey, fucker. I said get me a beer. The bar's that way." He tries to shift off of me, but once again stumbles.

"Make you a deal. You walk, and I'll get you one."

He offers me a big, toothy grin. One that says more serial killer than big happy guy.

"I changed my mind. I do like you now." He puts more of his weight on his own two feet. "Giddity up, pony."

"For fuck's sake, man. What did you drink?"

"About this many bottles of my buddy Jack Daniels." He splays his fingers in front of his face, lifting them each up before settling on what looks like three, but in reality, looks like that Star Trek nerd hand gesture.

"Come on. We're almost there."

Heavy footsteps come from behind, and Stone's weight shifts again. Twat Knot's head appears over his shoulder. "Come on, dumbass. Let's get you to bed."

"I specifically requested a beer, not a bed."

"Yeah, man. Whatever."

With TK's help, we finally manage to get him into one of the open rooms. He smiles when we get to the edge of the bed and plops down onto it.

"Nice place to pass out."

"Why don't you do that?" I advise. "You'd be doing yourself a favor."

Stone Face falls back, his massive body barely fitting. He looks more like an adult sleeping in a toddler's bed. TK and I stand back and watch as he shoves a tiny pillow under his moon sized head. His body goes slack when he finally passes out.

"I'm going to roll him on his side so he doesn't drown on his own puke," I say. "Get a trash can, will you?"

Stepping over to the bed, I try to roll his ass over, but it takes us both to manage it. Once we've got him settled, I slide the bucket on the floor beneath him.

That done, I take a step back and stare down at my friend. "The fuck you think's going on with him?"

"No clue. Been like this for a month or more now. Missing meetings, flaking on his assignments. Drunker than Otis on Andy Griffith."

Stone Face coughs out a choking gag. His body lurches before he spews like a fucking geyser, missing the bucket entirely.

"So glad we got him that bucket," TK drawls, pointing at the mess. "I'm not cleaning that up."

Stone Face shifts again, muttering and moaning, "Get away from my sister."

TK and I look at each other, confused. "Does Stone Face even have a sister?"

Twat Knot shrugs. "Dude, I know fuck all about the guy. He doesn't really talk much. Just grunts and knocks people's lights out when Judge tells him to. If he has a sister, that's news to me."

That realization sets me on edge. "Yeah, me too."

TK has a point, though. Stone Face has never been a talker unless provoked. He does what he's asked as a prospect and stays to himself most of the time. If he's got family, he's never mentioned them, which begs the question: How much do we really know about him?

LINDSEY

MAYBE I SHOULD HAVE CALLED FIRST.

I look around the kitchen at my Uncle Judge's house, but there's no sign of where anybody is. Natalie and Kevin, the teens my uncle had taken in to raise as his own, are nowhere to be seen, and neither is his girl-friend, Grace.

Taking out my phone, I shoot off a text to my uncle.

At your house. Where is everybody?

I wait a few seconds to see if he replies, but there's no dancing dots to indicate he's in the process of replying. In fact, nobody's replied to me since last night when I'd been talking to Blair.

Where is everyone?

I text Karma for the hundredth time.

At Judge's house. Please call me. I'm worried.

Grabbing the handles on my overnight bag, I carry it into the living room.

Uncle Judge's house isn't all that big. I'd once had a bedroom here, but now that room belongs to Natalie, which means my place will have to be the couch.

That nagging feeling that something's wrong grows stronger as I place my bag in the corner of the room before heading into the kitchen to make a quick snack.

After talking with Blair last night, I knew I just couldn't stay away another minute. I miss everyone here so much, and it's the weekend, so I figured a little visit might be exactly what I needed.

But now, nobody is answering. No Blair. No Grace. No Judge or Karma. Even Natalie and Kevin have grown radio silent.

A car door slams outside, and suddenly, fear consumes me. There's a reason nobody's answering. Something's happened. Something is wrong.

I press my back against the wall, staying out of view of anyone who may barge through that front door.

I have no weapon, and I hate guns. Though Uncle Judge had taught me how to shoot when I was just a kid, I refuse to carry one on my body or in my purse.

"Lindsey?"

My shoulders sag with relief at Karma's voice. Stepping out from around the corner, I catapult myself into his arms, forgetting all about his injuries until I hear him gasp when our bodies collide.

"Oh my God," I cry. "I've been so worried. Why haven't you gotten back to me? Where the heck is everybody?"

Karma puts me back on my feet. With his hands on my shoulders, he pushes me back so he can look me in the eye.

"What the hell are you doing here, Lindsey?"

I blink. "What?"

He raises his arm and rubs his hand along the back of his neck, his eyes wild. "You shouldn't fucking be here."

My emotions have been like a rollercoaster in the last few minutes alone. Worry, fear, relief, and now anger.

"Go to hell, Karma," I snap, turning to march out of the room.

Catching my hand, he yanks me back. "No, baby, listen. Trust me, I love that you're here. Hell, I've been dying to lay my eyes on that gorgeous face of yours, but it's not safe here. Shit's going down, and everyone's on lockdown at the clubhouse.

I frown. "Nobody told me."

"Because you were in Houston, safe. Not here where shit's getting real, fast."

"What's going on, Karma? Tell me. All of it."

"Not now. I was almost to the clubhouse when you

texted. I rushed over to get you out safely. I'll explain everything later."

I study him, taking in the worry in his eyes and the strained set of his lips.

"I missed you," I tell him.

Karma's expression changes in an instant. "Oh, baby," he breathes. "I've missed you like you wouldn't believe."

Taking a step toward him, I raise myself up onto my tiptoes. Even then, Karma still has to bend down just to kiss me.

I'd only intended to give him a quick kiss, but I should've known better. There's no quick kiss with this man. Our lips are like magnets, just like our hearts.

Karma's arms wrap around my waist as he takes control of the kiss. His heat surrounds me, his size making me feel so tiny. I've missed that too. Karma has always made me feel so small. Fragile, even.

My heart thrashes in my chest, and suddenly, everything he'd said about safety and lockdown disappears from my mind, and all I can focus on is him. Here. Now.

Winding my arms around his neck, I spear my fingers through his hair, gripping the strands in my fist so I can pull him even closer.

Palming me ass, he lifts me so my legs can wrap around his waist, not once breaking our kiss as he carries me over to the couch. My back lands against the cushions, and Karma's mouth is on my breast before I can process what's happening.

"God," I pant. "Yes." Karma's head swivels with the motion of his tongue, his eyes searing into mine.

"Pants off," he growls around the tiny nub of my nipple clamped between his teeth.

I'm already way ahead of him. My pants are undone, and I wiggle them down, careful not to rip my breast away from mouth.

He enters me in one swift motion, and I cry out when he goes as deep as possible, which is deep. But then he stops. Gripping my chin, he forces it up so we're staring into each other's eyes.

"You're mine, Lindsey."

I nod, and he moves slowly in and out.

"Fucking mine."

He's growling now.

"Mm-hmm," I moan as he pulls out again, only to slam back in, causing the couch to bang against the wall.

"Oh, God."

"Only fucking mine."

"Only yours," I pant.

He slams into me again and I reach down, my fingernails digging into his ass, holding him tighter against me.

"Please," I breathe.

Karma ravages my mouth with his, our lips a perfect fit. Our—

"What the fuck?"

Karma and I both freeze, and my eyes shoot across the room. Uncle Judge stands with his back to us, his hands clenched at his sides.

"I know I did not just walk in on you fucking my niece in my house, on the couch I sit on with my family," he declares, his voice eerily calm.

Karma's wide eyes meet mine, and I quietly place a hand over my mouth to stifle my giggle. Karma looks more afraid than amused, but I have to admit, as embarrassing as being caught is, Uncle Judge being the one to do it is pretty funny.

"Uh…" Karma pulls away from me, scrambling to pull up his pants that are hanging around his knees. "Judge, man, loo—"

Judge's hand goes up in the air. "You know what? I don't want to fucking know. I'm gonna go to the garage and see if I can find some bleach for my eyeballs. You two get yourselves together, and let's get our asses to the clubhouse, yeah?"

He sounds like he's going to be sick, and it's killing me having to hold in my laughter.

"Yeah, boss," Karma replies, but Judge is already gone.

Karma's head whips around. "I can't believe you're

fucking laughing." He's trying to be serious, but he's already grinning by the time he finishes the sentence.

When I open my mouth, the dam bursts, and I can't hold it back another second. A loud, soul-cleansing cackle erupts from my throat as I lay on the couch, with Karma joining me.

After a couple of minutes pass, and a few deep breaths to bring my mirth under control, I stand and pull up my jeans. I still can't wipe the smile off my face, though.

Once I collect myself, I move toward Karma, who places a kiss on the top of my head. "You're gonna get me fucking killed."

And then I lose it all over again.

KARMA

"WHAT ARE you smiling about over there?" TK smirks, handing me a couple of boxes of 9mm rounds to add to the stack in one of the side rooms we'd turned into a makeshift armory. Rows of rifles, hand guns, and piles of ammo pooled from various places around the clubhouse into one room. "You get laid or something?"

Oh, I did, but that's none of his damn business. I could've done without Judge walking in on us, but fuck, it was good. Felt like before shit went south between us. But even as happy as I feel right now, I know she's not ready.

"Can't a guy be happy?"

"Not if he's you. Seriously, did you get body snatched or something, man? I can count on one hand the number of times I've seen you smile, and I've known you for seven years. Shit's weird."

"Shit changes."

"You don't."

He heads off toward the bar where the rest of the guys are waiting on our brothers from San Marcos. They'd called a couple of hours ago to give us a heads-up that they were on the way. Houston and San Antonio were ready to hit the pavement, but had sent ahead a couple of guys just to have boots on the ground ready if shit went down in a hurry. The second they got here, Judge put them with the families at Blair's women's shelter, which was still being remodeled by GP on his off hours. With extra eyes on them, and being some place off the beaten path, I feel better about Lindsey being back here with shit about to go nuclear.

Part of me wishes she had stayed back in Houston, but after last night, I couldn't be pissed she came to visit. Especially if that Harry fucker she's been mentioning isn't hanging around her while she's worrying about her family. I'm not about to give that guy a chance to swoop in like a knight in shining armor. Fuck that shit. The second this is all over, Harry and I are going to have a little chat about who Lindsey belongs with, and it sure as hell ain't him.

Pulling out my phone, I shoot off a text to Lindsey. I hated leaving her last night, but we had shit to prepare for at the clubhouse, and I'm trying to give her her space.

You doing okay?

She replies almost immediately.

I'm good. Been helping Grace and Shelby get groceries for the clubhouse. Blair's watching the kids. How about you?

I smile as I type my reply.

That wasn't what I meant, baby. I'm good, tho. Judge wants to kill me again, so pretty standard day here.

The dots pop up and disappear again multiple times. Finally, her response comes through.

I don't know how I feel. Being home feels good and foreign at the same time. Why is Houston here?

For your protection.

I can almost picture her fingers flying over the screen as she types. She's been around this life long enough to know how bad it is when we call in help.

What aren't you telling me, Karma?

I consider my answer carefully. She's on the fence, I know that. Pressuring her isn't the way I should play this.

I know you may not be ready to hear this, but I love you. Please stay safe, and I'll see you when this is all over.

GP pokes his head inside the front door, calling out, "Cavalry's here!"

A reply chimes after I slide my phone into my pocket, going unanswered. Thinking about Lindsey can't be at the forefront of my mind with the fight ahead of us. If she knew the brevity of it, she'd be here pulling my ass out of the fight, and I'm not going to put our club down anymore members, no matter how far I am away from fighting condition.

Following the line of guys outside, we welcome the brothers. Their President, Ricochet, embraces Judge. He's a fucking monster, just like our Prez, and even older. I don't know what these old guys eat, but I can only hope to be in as good a shape as they are at that age.

"You look like shit. They not feeding you up here in Austin?" Piper, their enforcer, calls out from atop his bike. He and I go way back. Judge had sent me down there for a few weeks for added muscle during my first year as a patched member. I learned a lot from him. He was physically smaller than me, but outside of Stone Face, Piper could whip anyone's ass here, including mine.

I pat my stomach. "On a diet."

Swinging off his bike, he takes off his helmet and tucks it under his arm before making his way over with his hand out. I take it, giving it a firm shake.

"Good to see you, man. You doin' okay?"

"I'm here, aren't I? Can't be in that bad a shape." Patting him on the back, I nod toward the clubhouse. "It's good to see all of you. We're going to need all the help we can get."

It takes twenty minutes to get everyone inside, and find enough chairs for the table. The room is packed to the gills, and I fucking love the sight of it. Our numbers had been down for the last couple of years. Not that we aren't looking for new blood, but with our focus elsewhere, we'd dropped the ball a bit on it. It worked for us most of the time, but shit like this makes me glad we have brothers nearby.

"I want to thank Ricochet and San Marcos for joining us."

Ricochet lifts a chin in his direction. "Black Hoods stick together."

Judge straightens up at the front of the table. Try as he might, the strong front he's putting on has plenty of worry behind it. Our numbers are better, but the plan is shaky at best. He knows this, and so do the rest of us. These guys evade cameras. They'll smell a big score smoking gun a mile away. We have to have something better, or we'll be the ones going up in flames.

"I'm going to get straight to the point, gentlemen. We've got a mountain to climb. Fucking Everest. These guys have fire power, bodies, and for some fucking reason, the higher ground."

"I don't like to interrupt, but I might have something to help cut down on that," Piper offers, pushing up closer to the table.

"I'm all ears, brother. Floor is yours."

"We've got a guy on the inside. Prospect who took the fall for one of the patches. He's been in solitary for the last couple weeks, and we haven't been able to get in to see him. Ricochet called in a favor and got me in this morning before we rolled out after Judge mentioned the Ladrones."

"What's a prospect got to do with this shit?" Stone Face quips, a steaming cup of coffee in his hand. After yesterday's grand entrance, and a talk with Judge early this morning, he seems keener on doing his fucking job and filling his seat at the table.

"His roommate's an ex-Ladrone."

"Well, you have my fucking attention, Piper. What else you got?" Shit, he's got all of our attention. After weeks of this shit, we may finally have some fucking answers. Ones we regrettably couldn't find on our own.

"According to our prospect, the Ladrones have a new player backing them. Big time. Gave them the capital, extra bodies, and fuck ton of firepower."

"They get a name?" I ask.

"He didn't, but they're hitting garages everywhere and sending the parts over the border. Big market over there right now."

Fucking chop shops. South America has a big market for cars and parts. Groups as far as Chicago buy everything with wheels and runs around the auction sites in Texas, driving them straight over the border. I'd gone to one of those auctions a year or so ago when I was looking to buy a better car for Lindsey. Some guy bid me up to twice what it was worth. A truck parked next to it that should've been ten grand max, sold for almost fifteen grand to a group from Ecuador. I'd asked the auctioneer after the sale about it, and he'd told me it's been happening for years, but I hadn't connected those dots until Piper's intel.

The Ladrones were the wild card. It makes a hell of a lot more sense than just coming back here to reclaim their turf. There was nothing left when we hit them the last time. Absolutely fucking nothing. So to come back this hard, and with that many people, the backer angle cements the bigger picture together. Throw money at some street thugs and keep your hands clean. It has organized crime written all over it. The problem is, that question being answered only opens up a dozen more.

"Good information, but how credible is it?" Burnt inquires.

Judge starts to speak, but Ricochet jumps in. "I'd swear my life on it."

"But that gives us the who and the what. We're missing a key part here, and that's the where. We've got no location and an old-school plan."

"Hold your fucking horses, and I'll get to that part," Piper growls. "They were sent specifically to Austin to stir shit up, and they wanted you to get involved. The fact that y'all had bought a garage just sweetened the deal for them."

Judge furrows his brows. "Motherfucker. We're the fall guys. We get involved, and they stage it to look like we're the ones hitting them."

Motherfuckers is right. How deep does this go? Were the old guys just a ploy to get us involved, or was that the sheer design of their plans?

"That, I don't know. But with the past history y'all have with the old Ladrones group here in town, it makes sense," Piper continues. "Now the location may be the tricky part. All he could tell me was an old factory on the east side of town."

I frown. "There're dozens of those around here. It's a start, but we can't go sniffing around each one until we find them."

Judge nods to Hashtag.

"I'm on it." Hash is on his phone and out the door before the last word fully leaves his mouth.

"What's with him?" one of the San Marcos guys asks me.

"Tech guy."

He laughs. "Nerd."

"Pretty much," I say with a grin. "Guy knows his shit, though. He'll be like a bloodhound until he finds this place."

LINDSEY

BLAIR HAS DONE GOOD HERE. The old Victorian home her grandmother had left her is the perfect place for a women's shelter. It's also turned out to be a handy spot for the MC to hole up during whatever commotion we have going on right now. Plenty of space, and a place that no one would think to associate with the club.

"I need you to help Grace," Uncle Judge says, nodding his head in the direction of the kitchen. "Everyone needs food, places to sleep, somewhere to shower. Those kinds of things. She's helped before, and she could handle a single day thing, but she's never taken care of this many people for more than a meal or two. This was Marie's thing."

"I'm on it. The girls are all helping, so don't worry. Grace isn't alone."

Judge offers me a tight smile. "I'm glad you're home, kiddo."

"Me, too."

"But if I ever catch you touching any man on my couch ever again, I'll kill him."

I grin. "Noted."

Shaking his head, he pats me on the shoulder before walking away.

The house is packed. Every woman and child associated with anyone in the Austin chapter of the Black Hoods is staying here until the guys can get some undisclosed job done. There are also several folks from the neighboring chapters here as well.

I'm not gonna lie. It's nice to see the faces of so many old friends. But being crammed into Blair's women's shelter is not exactly ideal.

I head toward the kitchen and pick up a dish towel.

Everybody's working away at one task or another, but I choose to help Shelby by drying the dishes.

"I hear you gave your uncle an eyeful," Grace quips, looking up from the cutting board where she's chopping vegetables for a salad.

My face turns red. "You could say that."

"You and Karma?" Blair sounds equal parts surprised and pleased.

"Judge walked in on them," Grace informs her, along

with everyone else in the room. "They were on the couch."

"Atta girl," Shelby ribs, nudging me playfully with her shoulder.

Heat spreads through my chest. I've never been a prude, but I'm not one to discuss my sex life in front of a bunch of people.

"So does this mean you guys are getting back together," Grace asks, her face filled with hope.

"Not exactly."

Blair catches my eye, and I can tell she feels bad for me.

"Are you gonna move back home?" This question comes from a woman I've only seen around a few times. Her husband is one of the mechanics at the club's garage.

I gape at her. "I, uh… I don't know."

Just then, my phone rings. Saved by the bell.

But when I dry off my hands and pull the phone from my pocket, it lights up with Abe Frost's name. Shit.

I debate if I should let his call to go straight to voicemail, but everyone in the room is staring at me. I already have enough attention on me right now, and the last thing I need is to have to explain to a room full of women that my boss is a pushy old man with a bit of a God complex.

"Hello?" I step out of the room and into the alcove by the back door.

"Lindsey," Frost says, his tone not entirely unpleasant, but giving me uncomfortable vibes nonetheless.

"How are you?"

"I'm fine."

Frost clears his throat. "I just heard from Dr. Bardot that you have taken an undisclosed amount of time off for the foreseeable future."

Ah, now I understand. He just wants to know when I'll be back.

"Yes. And I do apologize, Mr. Frost, but we've had a bit of a family emergency here. I can't come back to Houston just yet, and I'm not one hundred percent sure at this point when I'll be able to."

"I see," Frost replies. "It does seem as if your family has had more than its share of emergencies of late, doesn't it?" His tone is filled with aggravation, which is strange in itself. I know I'm new there, but self-entitled rich kids with daddy issues comes in a distant second to my family.

"I'm sorry, sir?"

He chuckles, as if he'd been joking. But he and I both know he was accusing me of playing hooky.

"So when do you think you'll be back, Miss Sheridan?"

Okay, now he's pissing me off. "Like I said, sir, at this point, I'm not quite sure, but I'll be back to work as soon as the crisis has passed."

"I see," he repeats. "Well, please know that every day your away leaves the Institute understaffed and affects our top tier services. I would appreciate a daily update on your return to work status."

"Yes, sir," I say through gritted teeth.

Frost hangs up, and I stand frozen, my hand clutching the phone so tight, my knuckles turn white. I don't say this about many people, but I can honestly say that I hate that guy. Not only is he a skeevy pervert, but he's a total asshole too.

With a heavy sigh, I shove my phone into the back pocket of my jeans and return to my place at the sink beside Shelby.

"Everything okay?" Blair asks.

"Just my boss," I reply, picking a plate out of the drying rack and wiping it down with a tea towel. "He's kind of a prick."

"Good excuse to move home," Shelby teases.

I smile at her, but the whole idea of moving back here is overwhelming. For one, I have a career in Houston, and a great place to live. But here, I have family. Friends.

Karma.

"Are you at least planning on staying until this all blows over?" Blair asks.

Nodding, I grab another wet plate, avoiding meeting anyone's gaze.

"Yeah. I told my boss it may be a few days. I just hope Harry can hang on that long without me."

Knowing exactly who Harry is, and who Karma believes Harry to be, Blair snorts, setting off a round of laughter.

Laughter and friendship. A sure way to mend my heart just a little bit more.

KARMA

FUCKING HARRY.

I'll kill him, plain and simple. I don't give a shit if he's the nicest guy in the world. The fact that Lindsey is worried that he can't live without her makes me see red. Motherfucker won't see me coming, either. Trying to move in on my girl? Not in a million years am I going to let some little shit named Harry attempt to steal her away from me. My jaw clenches just thinking about it. What if something happens to me today, and she goes on to live a happy life with him?

I'd heard Lindsey and the others talking in the kitchen. I'd stuck around to see if they'd say more, but they didn't. Which is the only reason I'm not kicking the shit out of this *Harry* fuck right now.

Shut it down, man. Shut that shit down.

"Yo, Karma. You coming or what?" TK yells out over

the roar of idling motorcycles. Dozens of them are locked and ready to go, with our club at the helm. It had taken Hashtag about twelve hours to narrow down the location of the Ladrones hideout to an old flour mill. He'd gotten some thermal images from god knows where on that computer of his and confirmed a large group of people roaming around the property.

We wouldn't have given this place so much stock as an option, except for the fact that it had been closed for twenty years. It'd spent most of the last eighteen on the sheriff's sale, and only several months ago been sold to an offshore business. The pieces were all coming together, we just had to do our jobs today. Get in, get out, and end this shit.

"Nah. I think I'll stick around here."

"The fuck you will. Come on. One of the San Marcos prospects gassed up your truck for you."

"No need. I'm riding."

He sighs long and loud. "Judge know about that? Man, I don't know if today is the best day to be trying new shit out."

"Seems like the perfect day to me. We're going into this place with a new half plan. Why not roll the dice even more?" The smirk on my face is met with a look of disdain.

Right on cue, Priest rides up with my Harley Super Glide custom. She shines like a fucking beacon under the setting sun. Just gorgeous. Her deep blue paint job with the black and chrome accents gleam like she's a lady happy to be with her man again. I know I'm happy to see her. Lindsey used to say my bike was my first and only love. I'd normally argue with her, but she might be right today. I've missed this beautiful bitch.

"You think you're ready for this?" TK asks again.

"Shit's about to get dicey. If this is it for me, I'm taking my bike for one last ride."

"Right on, man. But if you lay it down on the way there…"

"If I lay down my bike, TK, I'll go ahead and spare you the need to come back and get me."

Judge steps out and surveys the sight in front of him. Brothers next to brothers. A beautiful view of chaos and brotherhood. When he eyes me hopping onto my bike, concern flashes in his eyes, but just briefly. he shrugs and trudges over to his own ride. He saddles up, and with a raise of his hand, the front of the group starts out after him.

My hand trembles as I reach for the ignition switch. A mixture of excitement, and a healthy dose of fear. She fires up the first try, rumbling between my legs like a faithful horse on a trail ride. I test out the weight of her, configuring my balance before popping the kickstand. I hit the gas lightly, letting her jerk forward. Shit, it's been too long. Sucking in a deep breath, I give her a little more gas and let her ease ahead. By the time I hit the edge of the driveway, my instincts take over.

Feeling the wind blowing against my face is like being hugged by your grandmother. Gentle, but soothing. If it weren't for the fact that we were charging headlong into a shitstorm of a fight, I'd have let myself enjoy it more. There will always be more time for this tomorrow, when all this shit's finally over.

The flour mill sits just off the main drag, giving us the chance to utilize back roads as our approach. A couple of the guys had gone ahead to scout out areas where we could ditch the bikes and head in on foot. We had options. None of them good, but options nonetheless. Forty-five minutes until the sun sets. Our cover for hopefully sneaking in undetected, blanketing us in the shadows.

A large building looms ahead of us in the distance. Ricochet peels off to the left with a group trailing behind him. The rest, including me, follow Judge. An apartment building that's seen better days comes up on our left, and he pulls into the parking lot. We wind our way around to a construction area that looks to be a new housing addition is being added into the area. He finds a secluded spot near several large modular trailers for the forums and kills his engine. Taking his lead, we all follow along until the last bike goes silent.

"We're going to go through the back lot, just behind

this build site," Judge whispers. "There's a field that sits adjacent to the mill. It'll give us the cover we need until we get close enough." He gazes at every one of us. "Take them out. All of them."

"Stay safe and kick some ass," TK cheers us on with a quiet laugh. The group breaks away and follows Judge's instructions, disappearing into the night.

Checking my side piece again, I feel someone grab my shoulder.

"I want you to hang back." Judge's face is stern and unmoving.

"You know I can't do that, Judge. Not in my nature."

"I had to say it for Lindsey's sake. If shit goes south, I want you to run. Get the fuck out of there. She still needs you, and so will Grace and the kids."

For the first time in my life, I see fear written all over Judge's face. He had someone at home to live for now, and the threat of losing what he'd just gotten back is rattling his normally stone-cold confidence.

"Don't give me this goodbye shit, Prez. We'll make it out of this. We're too stubborn to die."

"'Till the end."

"May the road rise up to meet you, Prez."

He disappears, and with a deep sigh, I follow my brothers toward whatever lies on the other side of the field. No one makes sound. The crickets are chirping, and the tall grass conceals us under the dark night sky.

The moonlight dips over the old factory. It's eerie, rusted beauty oddly draws me to it.

Shots ring out through the silence, shifting us all from the slow and methodical walk into a dead sprint. My heart beats with hard thumps against my sternum. Shouting now mixes in with the gunfire.

"Move! Move! Move!" someone shouts from ahead of me. "They know we're here!"

Bright flashes ahead of us in the night sky accompany the noise of the fight going on. My heart pleads for me to stop, but I ignore it. My brothers need me. Fuck what my heart wants.

The field comes to an abrupt end. Men run, scattering from all sides of the building, shouting and screaming. A teenager with his gang colors proudly on display charges toward me. TK raises his firearm and shoots him in the leg. He falls in front, screaming in agony. He's hurt, but he'll make it.

"They're fucking kids!" TK yells.

A smaller group of them skid to a stop when they see us approach, throwing their hands up in surrender. A little girl who looks like she's playing dress up, probably no older than Hashtag's kid, is dead center of them all.

"Please!" she screams. "I just want to go home."

"Get in the building," Judge orders. "We're not here for them. Get inside." A few of the guys break for the mill.

"Get out of here, all of you," I order the kids who take off, running in all directions.

We push on, heads down and guns forward. The mill's expansive grounds rock with an explosion on the left side of the property.

"The fuck is that?" I ask between gulps of air. My chest burns the harder I push myself, the pain radiating through every limb.

"That's Piper taking out their vans, cutting out their escape route. Come on," he huffs. "We have to keep going."

I shove the pain and exhaustion down deep, forcing my brain to ignore it. It'll work for now, but for how long?

I hear the sound of metal scraping. Focusing on where the noise is coming from, I see a large metal door slide open from the side of the mill, revealing at least a dozen men aiming their guns right at us.

"Get down!"

Reaching out, I grab hold of Judge's cut and drag him to the ground with me. We land on a thorn bush as the bullets whiz by our heads.

"Fuck! I'm hit!"

Priest falls to his knees, his hand clutching his shoulder. Army crawling over to him, I pull him into the bushes where I landed with Judge. Seeing the blood pumping from the bullet hole, I rip off a part of my T-shirt and place it over his wound, making him wince.

Grabbing his hand, I press it over the cloth, telling him, "Keep pressure on it." I turn my attention to Judge. "We're sitting ducks out here. We need to get inside, and fast."

"And how do you propose we do that?"

I search the area, looking for anything we can use as a shield from the firing squad. That's when I see the yellow exterior, shining like a beacon in the darkness.

"Can you drive a tractor?"

"The fuck you asking about a tractor for at time like this?"

I point over to an outbuilding where the door's slightly ajar. "Because there's one over there. Maybe we can use it as a battering ram to get inside."

Judge doesn't hesitate. "Fuck it. TK, you come with me. Karma, you stay here with Priest. We'll come back to get you."

The two of them stay low to the ground, running straight through the middle of the fight. TK gets caught up by a few, but Piper and a couple of San Marcos men come around the corner and take them out, allowing Judge and TK to slip inside the building while they take up guard position, picking off men as they approach. The sputtering of an old engine comes to life from inside, and I laugh. The fucking thing still works.

Piper and the guys run inside and shove open the doors, and within seconds, not a tractor, but a fucking bulldozer emerges, the radio playing that John Denver song about a country boy. Fitting, really, for what's about to come their way.

"That'll work," I chuckle.

Judge steers it toward the metal door. When our guys notice what we're doing, they fall in behind it, breaking free from their respective areas and Ladrones men. The engine hums louder the closer they get.

"Stay here," I tell Priest, pushing myself out of the bushes when they get close enough.

"Like I can go anywhere in this bramble bush."

Shifting it into the highest gear, Judge plows right into the partially opened door. The sickening screams and crunching in the wake of the bulldozer's destruction, where so many of the Ladrones stood firing at us, echoes out into the expansive hollow where machines once likely stood when the place was workable. Now, the area's littered with tents and makeshift homes put together for their newest recruits.

A group of six men open fire on us from above, the bullets pinging off the bulldozer's metal exterior.

Spying a staircase to our left, I holler, "TK, Piper, follow me."

We run for the stairs, taking them upward at a blistering pace. When we reach the top, the men don't even see us coming, their focus trained solely on our brothers below. I take aim and fire, sending one of them crumbling to the ground. Piper and TK hit their targets as well, leaving three. One of the remaining men fires at me, but misses by a mile.

"Not today, motherfucker," I seethe, returning fire. He's dead before he hits the ground. TK's already taken another guy out, and Piper's charging forward, shooting the last man standing in the leg.

"Where's your boss?" he screams at him.

"Fuck you, man."

Piper shoots him again near his femoral artery, spattering blood everywhere. "Not gonna ask you again."

"He's..." the man sputters as the life pours out of him. "The station house."

"Thanks, pal." Piper shoots, putting him out of his misery once and for all. "Did you guys see any railroad tracks outside?"

"I didn't. Best guess, they'd be over by the grain bins."

"Let's go."

We leave the way we came, giving Judge the rundown on the way out of the mill. The Ladrones litter the ground around us like a battlefield during the Civil War. Thankfully, no young faces among their casualties as far as I can tell. Kids, like the ones we came across earlier, see this shit on TV and think it's cool to be part of a gang until shit like this happens. It certainly gives them a healthy dose of reality, that's for sure.

"There," Hashtag calls out, pointing to the north side of the property. "Grain bins."

We move quickly, staying close to the mill as long as we can until the cover it provides disappears.

"Keep your eyes open," I tell the guys around me.

Seeing a small building just ahead between the bins, Judge surmises, "That has to be it." He orders the guys to his left, "Go around back. We'll take the rear."

We approach, but the gang leader from a few days ago comes out with a woman pressed tightly in front of him, his gun pressed against the side of her head.

"You take one step closer, I'll kill her."

"Why would we care about someone we don't know?"

"I'm pregnant!" she cries out, pulling back her sweater to reveal her protruding belly. Fuck. It's bad enough this fucking coward has a woman as his meat shield, but a pregnant one? That shit's lower than low.

"Let her go, man," Judge bellows. "It's over. Your guys are gone. No one's coming here to rescue you."

"That's where you're wrong, asshole. We have friends. Friends in high places. They already know what you did here, and they'll be coming for you."

Judge doesn't miss a beat. "Let them come. Doesn't change a damn thing about how this ends for you."

He cocks his gun, damn near pressing it into the woman's skull. She screams and squirms in his hold, begging for us to make it stop.

Judge takes a step forward, trying to get closer to the woman.

"I said don't move! I'll kill her. I swear I'll do it."

"We can't walk away from this, Prez. Not now," TK warns. "Just take him out."

"I can't with her there. He'll kill her before he drops."

"Come on, man," Judge tries to reason with him. "Let the girl go. It doesn't have to end like this for her."

The woman continues to struggle, and the leader's finger slips on the trigger. Judge aims, but a shot rings out over our heads. The whiff of a high velocity round buzzes by us, all before the woman screams and hits the ground, taking the gang leader with her.

Running over, Judge kneels down and asks her, "Where did you get hit, sugar?" while I check on our now dead friend. An entry point between his eyes is proof enough that he's not going to be a problem for us anymore. "Can you show me?"

She points to a spot on her shoulder, but there's nothing there. Just a small trickle of blood and rip in her shirt. She's damn lucky.

"You're okay. It's just a graze. Let's get you out of here."

Judge and I help her downstairs, where a couple of

the other guys take her off our hands. It's then when I notice Stone Face walking toward us with a sniper rifle thrown over his shoulder like fucking sack of potatoes.

"Sorry about the girl!" he yells out. "She moved on me. She okay?"

I have so many questions I want to ask, because I can't wrap my brain around what I'm seeing right now. Nevertheless, I force out the first one that comes to mind. "How in the fuck did you make that shot?"

"I was a sniper in the Marines," he replies with a shrug. He takes a look around and smiles. "Can we grab breakfast after this? I want waffles."

I shake my head at the crazy shit that just came out of his mouth. Sniper? Waffles?

"The fuck, man?"

The fuck indeed.

LINDSEY

THERE'S NOT a sober man in a two-block radius of the clubhouse after the guys get back. I listen with interest as they all tell their tales of who kicked whose ass, and who had taken out the biggest guy or saved some little kid. Everyone's stories were interesting, but a little bit different, depending on who told it.

The one story that stayed consistent no matter who told it, though, was the story of Stone Face going all Commando.

"Did you know he could shoot like that?" I ask, raising my voice so Karma can hear me over the excited chatter of multiple conversations and laughter.

He leans closer, his ear near my mouth. "What?"

"Stone Face. Did you know he could shoot like that?"

Leaning back, he studies me for a moment, and finally says, "You wanna get out of here?"

"And go where?"

"Home."

It's one word, but his eyes say so much more than that. *Our* home.

Swallowing, I nod.

Karma doesn't waste another second. He plucks the bottle of beer from my hand and places it on a nearby table, then leads me through the crowd.

Neither one of us says a word when we get outside. There are still plenty of people around, but Karma wades through them, a man on a mission, and heads directly toward his motorcycle.

"I thought you—"

Bending at the knees, he cups my face in his hands and presses his lips to mine, stealing my question, right along with the air in my lungs.

"Put your helmet on, baby."

Drawing in a deep breath, I stare up at him, my whole world spinning from that kiss. And then I put my helmet on.

I'd forgotten how much I love I riding on the back of Karma's motorcycle. From the instant he starts it up, feeling the power of the rumbling engine, I'm transported back to a time when everything between us was so much simpler, and so less complicated.

Wrapping my arms around his waist, I press my cheek to his back, holding back the overwhelming tears I feel building beneath the surface as he pulls out of the clubhouse's parking lot.

I've missed this. I've missed him. I've missed us.

By the time we've made the short trip to the home we'd once shared together, I've managed to settle my emotions for the most part. The wind helped dry the tears up at least.

After parking in the drive, he helps me get my helmet off. "Come on." Taking my hand, he leads me inside, and all I want to do is throw my arms around him and never let him go.

I don't know what I'd expected when Karma had asked me to come home with him, but I don't argue when he leads me inside and immediately up the stairs, straight into the bedroom.

He doesn't give me much of a chance to look around, but from what I can see, everything is exactly the same as I left it. He hadn't changed a thing.

Except for the graduation photo of me on his night-stand, framed front and center. The focal point of the table decor.

I hadn't given him a photo. That means Uncle Judge had.

We'd discuss that later.

"I know we're not there yet, Linds, but it feels so fucking good to have you back home."

"It feels good to be back," I whisper. The words are true, but they terrify me nonetheless.

This time when he kisses me, it's different. It's slow. Determined. Possessive.

There's no question that I belong to Karma and always have. But the way he lays me back on the bed only proves the issue. He knows just how to touch me. He knows exactly how I love to be kissed.

He consumes me. My head spins and my heart soars as our bodies move. I can barely catch a breath when he enters me, but who needs air when I have him?

He's my air. My reason.

We spend hours that way, giving and taking, and giving again. There are no words exchanged. We don't goad each other on or talk dirty like we tend to do. We just touch and feel and love. And it's perfect.

I fall asleep just as the sun is coming up, my cheek resting on his muscled pec, my hand draped across his waist.

We used to sleep like this all the time—before.

I don't know how long we lay that way. A few hours at least. And when I wake up, Karma has a single lock of my hair in his hand, twirling it around his finger.

I lift my head just enough to meet his gaze and smile. "Good morning."

"Morning," he says, his voice rough with sleep in a way that makes my toes curl. "Did you sleep okay?"

I don't look away from him when I say, "Best sleep I've had in months."

He stops twirling my hair and stares into my eyes, his face twisted with something I don't quite understand, and mutters, "Fuck it."

I'm suddenly on my back, watching Karma's perfectly shaped ass moving toward the dresser on the other side of the room.

He fumbles around with something I can't see and strides back to the bed, a man on a mission.

I sit up straight with the blanket tucked across my chest, held tight between my arms. "What are you doing?"

He drops to his knees beside me. He's naked and beautiful, and in that moment, more vulnerable than I've ever seen him.

He holds up his hand, and there, clutched between his thumb and fingers is a massive diamond ring.

And just like that, I can't breathe.

"Lindsey," he starts, but his voice cracks a little, so I gape at him as he clears his throat and tries again. "Lindsey, I know we're not ready for this, okay? So please, hear me out. Breathe through it and let me say what I need to say."

Hear me out. I know we're not ready for this.

The words play over in my mind as I stare at him like a deer caught in headlights, just trying to understand what exactly is happening right now. Then I realize he's waiting on a reply, so I bite my lip to keep from screaming and nod.

Karma takes a deep breath and shakes out his arms, releasing the tension from his body before he continues.

"Lindsey, I fucking love you. I know you know that, and you're it for me. There will never be another woman, ever, because there's only one you."

He turns his hand slightly and looks down at the ring he's holding. "Now this ring is ugly. Trust me, I know. But it was my grandmothers, and she's the only person, before you, that has ever just loved me. Like, truly loved me. And when she died, she left me this ring."

The ring is ugly. Hideous, in fact. But the meaning behind it transforms it before my very eyes.

"I want to marry you. I want to grow old with you. I want to be with you until the day I die, old and gray, beside the woman I love."

"Karma—"

He presses a finger to my lips. "Shut up, baby. I'm not done."

I can't help but grin.

"This is not a proposal, but a promise. I'm working so fucking hard to get better, Linds. I never wanted to admit it, but that one gunshot took so much away from me. I let it get as bad as I did, and that's on me. I lost you, and that's on me too. But I'm done with that shit. I'm done fucking up. I miss my girl, I miss my freedom, and I miss my fucking club."

Karma reaches for my hand and gently turns it until my palm's facing the ceiling. Placing the ring in the center of it, we both stare at the infinite circle. "I want to marry you more than anything, baby. I want the whole fucking world to know you're mine. I want to be yours, completely, but we're not ready yet. You're not ready yet. So I want you to take this ring and keep it close. Wear it around your neck, maybe, or carry it in your purse, and when you decide that you're ready for me to press this issue, all you have to do is hand it back to me. Will you do that?"

Oh. My. God.

I can't even see him for tears. He swipes his thumbs under my eyes, trying to stop them before they get too far.

"Babe, I can't keep up," he chuckles.

I sniff, trying to gather my thoughts. He'd just said so much, and I'm completely blank right now. So I say the only thing I can think to say.

"I will."

KARMA

THE DAY IS FINALLY HERE. My last day of therapy. The final test to see if I'm cleared. After testing my mettle against the Ladrones over two weeks ago, I'm feeling pretty fucking optimistic. It took a few days of recovery, but getting back out there and doing my job awakened the beast inside of me. I've been hitting the gym on my therapy off days with some of the guys. They still throw down more weight than I do, but I'm getting there every single day. It feels so fucking good to have my body respond to the exertion, the push and pull. The burn. I love every second of it.

Mentally, I'm still a work in progress. My talks with Blair really helped me see a lot of the things happening in my life were self-inflicted. Each session we've had together pushes me to see her opinion in a new light. A step in the right direction, she said, to getting what I want back.

My body.

My mind.

My girl.

My mantra the last few weeks? Get the first two, and work like hell to get the last one. I wasn't kidding when I made Lindsey that promise before she left to go to Houston. She was, and will always be, it for me. Even if she never gives me my grandmother's ring back, there'll never be anyone else to take her place. No one. I'd rather be alone than with someone who isn't her.

Helga brushes by my treadmill station with a wary eye trained on my movements and breathing. I hate to admit it, but she's growing on me. She's a tough bitch, don't get me wrong, but her kicking my ass a couple times a week has gotten me to this point. I may not have appreciated it before, but I do now. The comment about Lindsey was the kick in the ass I needed to make shit right.

My feet beat on the treadmill, one after another. My heart beats with heavy thuds against my chest, but the radiating pain and heavy breathing have moved into what Helga says is within normal range over the last few weeks.

"Keep going," she orders, her large fingers increasing the incline.

"You still trying to kill me, Helga?"

She shrugs. "Maybe I am, maybe I'm not."

I pick up the pace, meeting the increase at full speed. She eyes me cautiously, checking the heart monitor connected to my chest linked through Bluetooth to her tablet. Scrolling her fingers across the screen, she smiles.

"Ten more minutes."

She walks away, leaving me to my run. With each step, I repeat my mantra over and over again. The first two fade away, and I focus on the last one. My girl. Part of me wishes she could see me right now, pushing myself to finish strong, but showing her the discharge paperwork I hope to get today will be just as good.

The timer beeps on the treadmill, and I drop it down into a cool down, my heart racing in the best possible way. Bracing my hands on my knees, I work to catch my breath.

"Good, good," Helga deadpans. "Mm-hmm."

"Did I pass?" I force out between gulps of air.

She looks down at her tablet and scrolls around with her finger.

"Well?" I prod, wanting an answer.

"Just a minute," she grumbles.

"I ran almost twenty straight minutes and didn't keel over, woman. If that ain't passing, I don't know what is." Annoyance starts to prickle under my skin. This is my life she's got in her hands, and she's toying with it like an audience on the grand finale of one of those singing shows. I'll be damned if I have to wait after the commercial break to find out the goddamn winner.

"I swear to fucking Go—"

"Yes, you passed."

"Wait. Did you say I passed?" The shock is like a punch to the kidneys.

"I'll be sending over my report, along with the recommendation to your physician that you be released from all restrictions."

I reach out and pull her into my arms, hugging her like she's my coach at the Super Bowl as I bounce her up and down.

"Put me down," she orders, slapping my shoulders. I realize what I'm doing and put her back on her feet.

"Shit, sorry. Heat of the moment shit."

She straightens her navy-blue polo top, but smiles as she does. I wouldn't go so far as to say she's proud of me, but I think she is.

"When will I get the paperwork?"

"I'll send over my report today. Check with your physician in the next couple of days."

"Thank you, Helga. Thank you for pushing me."

"Sometimes that's all you need is a push in the right direction. Now get out and don't come back, you hear me?" she teases, waving her hand toward the door.

"Damn right I won't." I grab my cut and keys from

the assigned cubby for the last time. I don't look back when I step outside and take my first breath of freedom. I did it. I fucking did it. Relief, accomplishment, and a whole other range of emotions lift off inside of me. Fuck, is this how Lindsey felt the day she graduated? Regret creeps in at how I missed her day because of my selfishness. But if she gives me a second chance, I'll bust my ass every day to make it up to her until the day I die.

Pulling my phone from my pocket, I immediately call Lindsey. It rings multiple times before going to voicemail. It was a long shot that she would answer the first time since she'd be working at this time of day, but no reason not to try. I wait for the beeps and prompt to leave her message.

"Hey, baby, I got some news. I don't know how to tell you this…" I play it off. "They're clearing me, Lins. I did it. It feels fucking great, baby. I'm back. One hundred fucking percent. I wish you were here to see it." Elation fills me to the brim. "Listen, I know things between us aren't exactly settled, but I'd like to come see you this weekend. You could show me around Houston, maybe introduce me to Harry." That fucker will be long gone after I come to visit, I guaran-fucking-tee that shit. "Call me when you can. Miss you."

I hang up the phone and throw my leg over the seat of my bike. The looks I got riding up to the cardiac rehab center were priceless. Gaping mouths, wide eyes, and probably a bunch of fucking Karens with 9-1-1 on their speed dial. It would've been fun to mess with them more, but I never want to darken the door of this place again. Helga's orders and mine.

Flicking the ignition and popping the kickstand, I ride off toward the club and hopefully, toward fixing that last part of my mantra. Getting my girl back.

Chapter 29

LINDSEY

THEY'RE CLEARING ME, *Lins. I did it.*

I must have played Karma's voicemail message back ten times since my morning appointment had ended.

He's actually done it. For some people, that might sound like a big deal kind of statement, but they haven't met my Karma. He did it, and he'd needed to do it alone.

If there's one thing I've learned from all of this, it's that sometimes you need to love someone enough to take a step back and give them room to heal. And that's what both Karma and I had worked so hard on. And we'd both done it.

Kind of.

"So when my sister told me she had slept with him, I didn't even know what to say."

Vanessa Kingston is back in my office, again,

spouting off her usual superficial problems. I can't take it anymore.

I stare at her lips as she talks, but the words coming out of her mouth in a nasally, droning voice is driving me up the wall.

"Vanessa?"

She pauses mid-sentence. "Yeah?"

"You ever think you just need to stop being so damn spoiled? Go, get out from underneath the shade of your father's giant wallet and live your life, girl. There's so much more to it than what designer you're wearing and whose parents have more money."

She gapes at me, her mouth hanging open in shock.

I don't even care.

Placing the blank pad of paper on the table between us, I uncross my legs and stand, taking in the office. An office I never bothered to bring a single personal item into. It's just as stylishly austere as it was the day I got here.

Pulling open the bottom drawer of my desk, I retrieve my purse and stroll out of the room without another word to the misguided patient in the chair.

Abe Frost's secretary isn't at her desk, so I head straight for his office. I don't know why I feel so rushed, but it's like my heart can't keep up with my feet. All I want to do is get my things and get the hell out of here once and for all.

"I quit," I announce, swinging open his office door.

Abe's brows rise so high, I swear the stray hairs would brush along the ceiling. "I beg your pardon?"

"You heard me. I appreciate the opportunity of working here at the Institute, but if I have to sit for another minute and listen to one more blonde little rich girl complain about her sugar daddy's sexual proclivities, my head will explode. I thought this was the job for me, but I was wrong."

Abe stands as I speak, making his way around the desk.

"Miss Sheridan, surely there's something—"

"There's not. Now, if you don't mind, I'll go and collect my things. But I would appreciate it if you could have my check ready for me to pick up in an hour."

"I most certainly cannot," he chuckles, stating just how foolish he feels the request is.

"Yes, you will, or I'll tell the world about how inappropriate you are with your staff. And for all I or anyone else knows, it's the same with the clients."

"I'm never inappropriate with the clients," he seethes.

"Good. Then I'll be back in an hour to collect. See you then."

I stroll out of his office, tamping down the need to giggle uncontrollably. I can't believe I just did that. Oh my God. I'm never going to get another job ever again.

I giggle louder.

Once I make it to my condo, I rush around the rooms, packing up clothes, books, and photographs, loading them all into the backseat and trunk of my tiny car.

I don't stop for one second to think about what I've just done or what I'm about to do.

The last thing to be taken to the car is Harry.

Placing his bowl gently on the floor beneath the passenger seat, I wrap it tightly in towels and put packing bags all around it so it won't shift.

Once he's secure, I turn and look at the lake one last time.

Getting behind the wheel, I head over to collect my final paycheck before returning this god-awful ring to my soulmate.

Chapter 30

KARMA

THE PARTY'S ROCKIN' by the time I make it to the clubhouse with the ice we needed for the coolers. Normally, it would be a prospect's job, but we're running low on those after our unanimous vote this morning. They'd done a lot for this club, proved themselves, and it's only right they get a piece of the pie by becoming patched in members. With V finally out of the hospital, we were able to throw them the party to go with it.

I toss the bag of ice over my shoulder and stalk inside. The place is filled to the brim with my brothers, families, and a lot of fucking club girls. Patch parties always seem to bring them out of the woodwork, like there's some beacon in the sky for new patches needing old ladies. But it's a good fucking day to see my club expanding. If this run-in with the Ladrones taught us anything, it's that we need more members.

"About time you fucking got here," GP calls out from behind the bar. "Drinks are getting warm."

"That's never stopped you before, man."

"Ain't that the truth. Bring it back here. I dragged the coolers in for a re-stock."

Switching gears and heading toward the bar, I toss the bag of ice onto the countertop, letting GP fill the coolers behind him. As he does so, I lean against the bar, taking it all in. A few months ago, shit like this may not have happened for me. The dark spiral I was in would've killed me one way or another. To be here, celebrating new patches and my full recovery is a good fucking feeling to have in my book. The only thing better would be if Lindsey had come down.

Retrieving my phone from my pocket, I check for messages. Since my voicemail, I haven't heard from her. Feeling a little disappointed, I stow it back into my cut pocket. I've been trying to rationalize that she might be busy, or that I pushed too hard to stop myself from riding up there and searching the entire fucking city until I found her. That's what I would've done before, but she's changed, just like I have. Pressing my luck now might trigger her to the point she'll push me away again. That's not something I think would ever recover from. Time is all I have now, and I'll give her as much as she needs.

"Want a brew?" GP asks, popping his head up from behind the bar.

"Is it warm?"

"The fuck you think, K?"

"I'll pass, man. Warm beer is your thing, not mine."

TK shoves in next to me and reaches his hand out. "If he doesn't want it, I do."

GP slides one over to him, and he pops the top on the edge of the bar.

"Got some hotties here tonight, man. I'm gonna be a busy guy. Thinking that blonde over there with the big tits and juicy ass might be the first one." He points over to a girl, no older than maybe her mid-twenties, playing with her hair while she tries to flirt with Judge. Grace notices and shoves her way into the conversation, like a good old lady should.

"Doubt she'll be here long by the looks of it, man."

"Meh. There's more where that came from." His eyes trail after one of the ladies with a skirt barely covering her flat ass trying out her catwalk. Fucking patch bunnies. He takes a drag off his brew and leans over to me, the smell of hops saturating his breath. "Maybe that one and her friend. It's like a fucking buffet of pussy out there."

"You and I have a different idea of what a good pussy buffet looks like. It's a straight-up Sizzler out there." Not to knock the ladies present, but the old ladies have zero to worry about tonight. Zero.

"Doesn't matter who it is with me. I'll have a good time either way when I break in V and Priest's rooms later."

"You're doing what?" The lines forming between my eyebrows meet his sheer happiness. I must've heard him wrong, because if he said what I think he did, Hashtag is going to kill him. Fuck, I'd help him do it.

"Yeah, K. I do it to all the new patches," he admits with a smile. "My present to them."

I shake my head, trying to wrap it around how he hazes the new guys.

"You do this to everyone?"

"Fuck yeah, man. Hash's patch party was the best one. Threesome," he enunciates clearly with two fingers raised in the air. "It was fucking epic. Might see if I can make it a repeat tonight."

"You do know that Hashtag's old lady left the night of his patch party because she thought she walked in on him fucking around on her, right?"

His mouth gapes open. "Aw, fuck."

"Yeah. I don't think fuck sums that up, TK." Not even close. Hashtag lost years with his old lady and his kid because of that night. If he knew Twat Knot had done it as a prank, there'd be a funeral.

"You're not going to tell him, are you?"

"Depends. Knock that shit off, and I might forget about it."

"Yeah, man. I think I'm going to head back to the party. You sure you won't say anything?"

I shrug. TK's face is white as a fucking sheet. I get the feeling his streak will be ending tonight. When the time is right, I'll tell Hashtag and let the two of them sort that shit out, but for tonight, I want to enjoy seeing my club together again.

My phone vibrates, and it takes all I have not rip it out of my pocket like a kid on Christmas morning finding their presents. It has to be her. It just *has* to be. Looking down at the white text on the dark background is a fucking alert from the ESPN app, reminding about an MMA fight I'd been interested in. My happiness gets stomped on by my phone. Never thought I'd see that day. I'm turning into fucking Hash with his techy shit.

Giving up on the idea of her coming, I decide to join my brothers who've retreated outside, away from the bunnies, but I never make it there. No sooner do I step outside, I find Lindsey leaning against her car. She came.

"Lins?" I call out to her, approaching cautiously. She comes toward me at a steady run, leaping into my arms. "Baby, what's wrong?" I wrench her arms away from around my neck and pull her face up to me. "Come on, talk to me."

"I made a mistake."

"You're going to have to give me more than that."

"I should never have left that night."

My heart starts to flutter inside my chest. "You don't have to apologize for that, Lins. We're past all that."

"No, not that night," she corrects herself. "When you gave me this." She pulls my grandmother's ring hanging from a golden chain around her neck from underneath her shirt. "I thought Houston was what I wanted, but I realized something today. Austin is where I belong."

"I like what I'm hearing, Lins, but I don't want you to give up what you have there because of me. You're making a life for yourself."

"You don't get it, do you? Karma, I want a life with you. I always did, and I was just too scared to admit that. I'm miserable in Houston. I have been since I left." Moving her hands to the back of her neck, she releases the clasp on the necklace and removes the ring. "I want this life. I want you." Her delicate fingers wrapped around the ring, she places it in my hand.

"You're sure about this? I need you to be absolutely sure, because I can't lose you again."

"You're my end game too. I love you, Karma."

"I love you, baby. Always have, always will."

The ring in one hand, I wrap the other into her hair, pulling her against my lips. We crash together, a tangle of us melding in the heat of the moment, letting the past go.

It's a moment I'll never forget for the rest of my life. The day we came back for each other.

"Shit," she murmurs against my lips. "I forgot about Harry. He's in the car."

Pulling away from me, I frown. "Harry? Why the fuck is he here?"

"Why wouldn't I bring him?" Starting back toward her car, I watch as she opens the passenger door, grinding my teeth as she picks up a small bowl from the seat and tucks it under her arm.

"Meet Harry," she giggles, beaming up at me. "Harry, meet Karma."

Holding up the bowl, I look in at the little goldfish blubbing at me with its big eyes.

Fucking Harry.

STONE FACE

Flashing sirens pierce the night sky. Looking in my rearview mirror, I watch the police cars multiply. I can't control my grin.

Come get me, motherfuckers.

I make a left turn, counting at least eight cop cars following at a safe distance. Their lights are flashing, their sirens are wailing, and I'm pretty sure one of them is saying something over the loudspeaker, but there's too much noise for me to make out the words.

Tipping back my bottle of beer, I swallow what's left and toss the empty into the passenger seat. I have three more full ones sitting right there beside it, and I don't plan to pull over until every last one of them is empty.

I snag one out of the box while scanning the dashboard, searching for the switch that flips on the lights and sirens in this police car.

The same police car I'd climbed into thirty minutes ago at the local Turbo Gas while the police officer had been inside. The stupid son of a bitch never should've left his keys in the ignition if he didn't want the damn thing stolen.

The car swerves, and I snap my head up just in time to avoid slamming into a curb. *Shit.* Almost spilled my fucking beer.

Once I'm back in my lane, I find the switch to turn on the lights and a dial to control the siren. I flick the lights on, and when the word *wail* catches my attention, I turn the dial directly to it and the car does just that. It wails.

Up ahead, I see the lights of the clubhouse, knowing tonight was the patching in party. I'd been on my way there when I found this car, and I knew in an instant I wouldn't be attending. But I could do this.

Fumbling with the microphones beneath the siren activation switch, I yank off the one labeled PA and get ready to give my boys a treat.

Slowing, I lower the speed to a mere ten miles per hour. Laughter consumes me when I see that two more police cars have joined my procession. I lead them all, my windows open, my music cranked, and my sirens wailing just as loud as theirs.

One by one, people flood the sidewalk at the side of the clubhouse. Partygoers and club members alike have come to see what the fuck's going on out here.

It's me. I'm what the fuck is going on.

"Hello, motherfuckers!" I scream into the PA.

Fingers point and eyes widen as I slowly pass them by. Judge steps out of the crowd, the others hot on his tail. Twat Knot's laughing his ass off, raising his fist in the air in solidarity. I raise mine back out of the driver's side window.

"Have a drink for me, asshole! Looks like I won't be having one for a while."

———

Read more about Stone Face's story in Dark Destiny.

THE SERIES

About the Authors

Avelyn Paige is a USA Today and Wall Street Journal bestselling author who writes stories about dirty alpha males and the brave women who love them. She resides in a small town in Indiana with her husband and three fuzzy kids, Jezebel, Cleo, and Asa.

Avelyn spends her days working as a cancer research scientist and her nights sipping moonshine while writing. You can often find her curled up with a good book surrounded by her pets or watching one of her favorite superhero movies for the billionth time. Deadpool is currently her favorite.

———

Want to talk books? Join Avelyn's Facebook group to learn about new releases, future series, and to hang out with other readers.

ALSO BY AVELYN PAIGE

The Heaven's Rejects MC Series

Heaven Sent

Angels and Ashes

Sins of the Father

Absolution

Lies and Illusions

The Dirty Bitches MC Series

Dirty Bitches MC #1

Dirty Bitches MC #2

Dirty Bitches MC #3

Other Books by Avelyn Paige

Girl in a Country Song

Cassie's Court

About the Authors

Geri Glenn writes alpha males. She is a USA Today Bestselling Author, best known for writing motorcycle romance, including the Kings of Korruption MC series. She lives in the Thousand Islands with her two young girls, one big dog and one terrier that thinks he's a Doberman, a hamster, and two guinea pigs whose names she can never remember.

Before she began writing contemporary romance, Geri worked at several different occupations. She's been a pharmacy assistant, a 911 dispatcher, and a caregiver in a nursing home. She can say without a doubt though, that her favorite job is the one she does now–writing romance that leaves an impact.

Want to talk books? Join Geri's Facebook group to learn about new releases, future series, and to hang out with other readers.

ALSO BY GERI GLENN

The Kings of Korruption MC series.

Ryker

Tease

Daniel

Jase

Reaper

Bosco

Korrupted Novellas:

Corrupted Angels

Reinventing Holly

Other Books by Geri Glenn

Dirty Deeds (Satan's Wrath MC)

Hood Rat

Printed in Great Britain
by Amazon